An Experimetal Childhood

Boyhood adventures amidst a farming revolution
in Scotland in the 1950s

Alan Reid

In 1952-3 dramatic change was taking place in farming. Oil lamps gave way
to electricity, horse and steam power to tractors, hand sheep shearing to
mechanical clipping and hand to machine milking. It was a time when self
sufficiency was crucial as strict post WW II rationing was still in place.
Through the eyes of a nine year old, Alan Reid tells these stories with
nostalgic love for a time, pre television, when he and his friends made their
own amusement with great ingenuity and sometimes dramatic consequences.
Each day was a welcome challenge to find new excitement. A truly
experimental childhood.

First published in 2016 by

Amazon Createspace

A catalogue record for this book is available from the British Library

ISBN-13: 978 1540454676
ISBN-10: 1540454673

Designed and edited by Garf Collins

For George Leven

with whom I shared
these carefree times

Contents

Introduction

In the early 50s, just after the war, there was relief that the war was over but also great anticipation for what the future might hold. Lots of people emigrated to get out of Europe. Some of my family did.

There was a revolution taking place. A transition from carthorse and steam engines to tractors and electricity. From oil lamps to electric light and local knowledge to general knowledge due to the advent of the new medium of Television.

I have written these short stories in the form of a weekly and seasonal diary of life as seen through the eyes of a youngster - a naive youngster.

My stories concern the everyday life of an eight or nine year old boy, living on a hill farm in Southern Scotland in the early Fifties, helping on the farm and playing with my mates. Birds nesting, rabbiting and all the things we got up to on the farm as kids.

Hopefully this will give an insight into life as it was then. Remembering all this has led me to reflect on how much has been lost in farming today.

The Back Kitchen.

The farm nestled behind a small wood in the foothills of Southern Scotland, roughly halfway between the highest points; Queensbury in the lead hills and the sea at the Solway Firth. The river Ae cut through the countryside, all the way down to the Firth, meandering through the silver birch and fir trees rising up from its banks, enhanced by a carpet of heather and bracken that encroached upon the surrounding hills. In the river slimy green boulders, embedded like stepping stones, protruded out of the water, water that never ceased babbling, unless enraged by a sudden storm. There was a single track railway line that ran from Dumfries to Shieldhill, Lochmaben and onwards, following the contours of the river.

Our farm - Hightown of Tynwald - was a mile and a half from Shieldhill. That's where I went to school, with eight other pupils, in the late forties and early fifties. This was our stamping ground. There was George, the teacher's son from Shieldhill. The Telfer boy's, Austen and Robert from the next door farm Fernieclough and Graham Kirkpatrick from Shieldhill. Sometimes at the weekends in the summer, Tim Martin from Lochmaben and Bobby Wilson from Lockerbie would appear, but mostly it was George and me. He more or less lived at our Farm and was part of our extended family. Base Camp was the back kitchen. When returning from our forays, you couldn'ae beat walking up the cobbled yard towards the back kitchen door, to the smell of scones, tattie soup or rabbit stew.

Mum and Aunty May would be busying themselves, setting out the table and getting ready for dinner, with pots and pans steaming on the range and tarts and scones in the oven.

"You boys wash your hands at the spicket and take yer boots off afore you come in" Mum would shout.

"Aye, wash yer hands. Right now," Aunty May, would chirp, echoing Mums words.

Mum used to bang an old galvanized bucket that sat outside the back door, with a poker. A signal to the men folk that dinner was ready and she did'nae have to bang it twice when it concerned food. The men would appear from wherever they had been working and stroll up the yard to the back door, washing their hands at the spicket, taking off their tackity boots afore going in for dinner.

"Won't be a minute" Mum would say.

"Aye, dinner won't be a minute." Aunty May would echo, singing a little Scottish song, which always finished off with a shriek, as she moved like a Dervish dancing around a camp fire, with one arm full of soup plates and a flashing ladle in the other. She said that it was like that when she danced the Eightsome Reel when she was young, then carried on busying herself at the range.

There was always at least half a dozen of us for dinner and food for many more. We were often joined by casual workers or the odd salesman like Willie Hall, who, when in the area, would always turn up just before dinner, knowing there would always be a place for him.

We would all settle down in our places and, if there wasn't

enough room, the old wooden table had an extension above the knife draw that could if need be make it bigger. The soup was ladled into our plates and you could always have another helping if you wanted. Aunty May said there was no bottom in that soup pot. Then it would be stew, usually rabbit, but sometimes beef or mutton. You had to watch the rabbit stew, because usually they had been shot and sometimes you would get a pellet stuck in your teeth. We always had lots of veg, tatties, cabbage, tumshie and carrots. Then it was apple or rhubarb tart with thick custard. Mum always cut an extra slice of tart,

"In case Willie comes" she'd say. We called it Willie's slice and when Willie didn't turn up it caused more trouble than you could imagine. Mum and Aunty May would set their food aside and eat it after every one had gone back to work.

Dad always had a cat nap after dinner, 'Just ten minutes.' Everybody else would be sitting around the table having a chat and a cup of tea and, if Willie or no one else turned up, we would all be looking at 'Willie's slice' sitting on its plate in the middle of the table. Everybody knew it was up for grabs but we all kidded on we didn't know it was there. But one slight movement was enough, just a twitch and everybody went for Willie's slice like hounds to the kill and it was gone. I'm sure Mum cut an extra slice just for the crack. Things always settled down after that and there was lots of chat and banter.

The men would tell us where to look for bird nests and if there were any rabbits or rats we could get with the dogs and ferrets. Then it was back to work for the men. Dad would wake up and the men would start to shuffle about and put their boots back on and roll a fag before starting off back down the yard to their work, farting on each step, trying to outdo each other, with a sly grins on their faces.

"Dirty buggers" Mum would say, looking out of the kitchen window above the sink, while putting the dirty dishes in to soak.

"Just terrible. Just terrible." Aunty May would say, thinking Mum was talking about the mess that she was cleaning up after the fight for Willie's slice.

That's how things were in those days, not long after the War. Nobody had much money, so nobody talked about it.

They were just glad to be alive and free. They mourned the few friends that had failed to make it back home and everyone was happy to help anybody who needed it. Shirkers were not welcome and would definitely get a boot up the arse if they encroached in our part of the World. Dad would see to that.

The really good thing about living on the farm was that there was always plenty of grub. I think that's why everything revolved around the Back Kitchen.

The King dies

On Monday morning it was off to school. It was about a mile down the road on the outskirts of Shieldhill and about half a mile from the railway station. Mrs. Leven, the school Mistress, who was George's Mum, ruled everyone with a rod of iron. All nine of us except George. His Dad had died a couple years earlier and since the age of seven, George had been the man of the house and got away with murder. That's why I think his Mum was glad he palled up with me and he spent more time on the farm with us than he did at home.

It was the 6th of Feb 1952 and something had happened. You could tell. Folks seemed to be looking at one another hoping for any tidbits of information they could glean. George and I had just got back from school and it seemed an adult kind of thing, so we went into the Back Kitchen to get a drink and sandwich. Mum and Aunty May were there preparing dinner. I think Aunty May had a tear in her eye.

"What's up Mum," I asked and George piped in, "Yea, What's up."

"Oh it's just terrible, just terrible, the Kings dead and such a wonderful man" Aunty May more or less echoed her words,

"Aye the Kings dead, the Kings dead. Just a wonderful man and he's dead boys."

Mum went on. "But Liz will be Queen and she's just a bairn.

"Just a bairn. Long live the Queen" Aunty May wailed.

The next day when we went to school, we had to stand in silence for a minute.

"A sign of respect." Mrs. Leven said. She then went on to explain all about why there was a Monarchy and what it meant. It was all very somber but we didn't mind. Iit was better than lessons.

The thrashing machine

While walking back from school that afternoon, we could hear the thrashing machine working down at the Connells farm. It was due at our place next and George and me couldn't wait. It was always fun when the thrasher came to thrash the corn. The rick yard had twelve ricks in it. Six down each side. The thrasher would go down the middle of them with a rick on each side, so they didn't have to move it so much and we could kill rats like we did last year.

The next day when George and me were walking back from school we heard the commotion of the steam engine coming up the road from the Connells farm, to set up at our farm, for the next morning. There it was the steam engine, all steam and clanking, a whiff of coal smoke wafting down the road, as it was puffing away, pulling the thrasher, the baler, the work means' wooden caravan and a little dark blue van with little oval windows in the back doors. It seemed a mile long.

We ran up the road after it, shouting and squealing. It was all noise. When we got near the farm, Old Nell the collie and Chips the Terrier ran down the road to meet us to see what all the noise was about. Painted in big red and green letters on the wooden sides of the thrasher were words;
James Kingan and Son.
Threshing Contractors.
South of Scotland.
They unhitched the thrasher and ran it down the middle of the rick yard to the bottom two ricks, to be ready for the morning. Dad and Barnsey put the baler onto the back of the thrasher with the old Standard Ford car and chocked up the wheels to stop it rolling about. They then turned the steam engine around facing the thrasher and put the big belts on all the different flywheels and spindles, ready for the morning. After a test run they damped down the fire under the boiler.

As usual the crew was old Nughy the dogsbody and Jimmy the engineer. They had it down to a tee and probably did the thrashing on twenty or thirty different farms every year. So they knew what they were up to. They also knew everybody's business in the South of Scotland as well.

"There nothing like a little chit-chat after dinner and hanging out everyone's dirty washing." Jimmy would say giving Dad a wink. Nughy had lost two fingers since last year. Apparently he was working on the circular saw at Kingans Sawmill, when he got one finger cut off shoving a bit of wood through the saw. When Mr. Kingan said,

"How the hell did you do that Nughy," he got a bit of wood, went over to the saw and said to Mr. Kingan,

"I just did that Mr. Kingan," and cut another finger off.

After that he was nae allowed to work on the circular saw no more.

"I sometimes wonder if one day I'll see him come out from the binder all mixed up with the corn and chaff." Said Jimmy with a sly grin.

The labour for working the thresher came from the surrounding farms. There were usually three or four of them and our lot. When it was other farms turn for the thrasher, we would send one or two to help.

When the weather was bad, or it was the weekend, Jimmy and Nughy would go back to their homes in New Abbey, in the little blue Van.

The next day George and me had to go to school. We couldn't wait for four o'clock to come round, so we get back to the farm and get mucked in with the men.

When we got back home after school, the yard was fair buzzing. There was smoke, steam and belts flying around, with the thrasher making a deep hum as the sheaves were fed in. The balers ram was boom booming and folk were busy everywhere. They had done nearly two ricks and when they got to the bottom they would move everything up to the next two ricks, ready for the morning. There were loads of rats in the last few sheaves and every sheaf had a rat under it. The dogs were going mad. Even Sandy the cat was sitting there waiting to see what was up for grabs but keeping an eye on the dogs in case they gave chase. That was one of our favourite sports, when there was nothing else to do, chasing the cats with the dogs. But with so much going on, I think even they had declared an amnesty for the thrashing season.

George and me were supposed to be dragging great big bags of chaff into the barn but it was more fun hunting rats with the dogs. When it came to the last few sheaves it was mayhem. Rats everywhere. The dogs didn't know which ones to go for next. All the men had their trousers tucked into their socks and were hitting them with their pitchforks or trying to stamp on them with their hobnailed boots. Lots of them got away into the next door ricks but we knew we would get them later. When the men finished off the thrashing for the day, the whole lot was moved forward to the next ricks ready for the next day. The casual workers from the neighbouring farms went back home to feed their beasts and do the milking.

After the thrasher was set for the morning, we gave Barnsey a hand with the milking. We weren't good enough to do the milking ourselves. It took us ages to fill a luggy but Barnsey could fill a luggy in what seemed like a couple of minutes. We could feed the cows, muck out and put some bedding down

Mum and Aunty May had the dinner on usually for about six o clock. The thrasher men always had dinner with us. It was a sort of carnival atmosphere - plenty of banter. They would chat till nine o clock or later. I don't know how they managed to get up the next morning, but they always did. They always had the steam engine fired up and ready to go before we went out to school.

The old ricks were disappearing every day and so were the rats. After a few days all the thrashing was over and the rick yard was just a yard again. Jimmy and Nughy moved onto the next farm. We wouldn't see them again till next year.

Sledging on the Hill

The bales were all stacked. The corn was bagged and the chaff was all loose at the end of the barn. The barns were full and the yards clean and empty. Life settled back down to normal, or as normal as could be. It was just milking the cows, feeding the sheep and watching the weather in case it gets bad and the cows and sheep get stuck up the hill, like some sheep did last year.

Last year we had about twenty sheep stuck up the back of the hill. The Old Man (what we sometimes called Dad) had to drag a bale of hay up to them every day for a week. He made a sledge out of an old corrugated tin sheet, by bending up the front and spiking a hole through the tin and putting a rope through to pull it. Sometimes on the way back, if it wasn't too steep he would sit on it and sledge down, to save walking in the deeper snow. That's where Brother John, learned a lesson, or should have.

Dad wanted to take two bales of hay up to the sheep and we were asked to give a hand. There was George and me and my brother John, who was four years older than me and a lot stronger than us. We pulled the sledge up the slopes and the Old Man walked behind acting as a brake man, making sure the bales didn't fall off and when we stopped for a rest, from time to time, he would stick his big knobbly herding stick in the snow to stop the sledge slipping back down the hill. Some places were so steep we could only take one bale at a time, take one off, get over the steep part and go back for the other one. When we finally made it to where the sheep were marooned, we broke open the bales and scattered the hay to feed them. They were glad to see us and it was a hive of activity there as they munched their hay. Although it was up the hill, it was in a sheltered spot out of the wind. They were probably better off than the sheep down near the farm where there was mud to contend with.

After the Old Man had checked the sheep to make sure there were no weak or injured ones, it was time to start back down the hill. Brother John said we should sledge back down. The sledge was about eight foot long, just a sheet of corrugated tin with a rope either side. When riding on the sledge it was like pulling on the reigns while riding a horse. If you pulled the rope one way, it would turn that way. The only slight defect was lack of brakes. But you could stick your feet out into the snow to slow you down, if need be. Well John wanted to steer so he got on the front so he could hold the reigns and be in control, but he kept sliding off the front, because the hill was too steep, so we turned it sideways a bit and John got on and wrapped the ropes around his feet to stop him slipping off while Dad held the sledge ready for take-off.

John lay back in the take-off position. George and me got on the back and snuggled in behind John and the Old Man swung the sledge round and we were off. It went off like a rocket and it hadn't gone fifty yards before George and me abandoned the sledge. I think John would have done the same but for one thing. He had put the ropes around his feet and couldn't get off. It was getting steeper and steeper. We picked ourselves up and watched John. I thought he was showing off going like a bat out of Hell towards a five wired fence-some of it barbed - at the bottom of the hill. That's when he hit the snow covered ruts, made by the tractors over the years. A bit like a ski jump.

He took off like an aeroplane, doing a victory roll as he went clean over the fence and into the field that ran up to the Steadings farm. Even Dad stood there looking on in amazement at John's bravado.

The sledge finally came to rest in the middle of a great pool of melt water and sank with John still on it. The water was only about a foot deep. John tried to get clear but had one foot tangled in the rope and fell over in the ice cold water. The Old Man didn't worry too much about John, when he saw him get up and start running for the house.

"He couldn't be hurt too bad if he could run like that." He muttered. George said,

"It's a good job he tied himself on, or he might have fallen off and hurt himself."

The snow started melting after that and we got the sheep off the hill a couple of days later. John had a few bruises and a bit of hyperthermia. Otherwise he was ok but he did hog the fire for a bit. So the lesson John learned was;

'Don't tie yourself to an inanimate object at the top of snow covered hill'

Dancing at school

Back to school and Mrs. Leven had decided it was time to teach us all how to dance. She said it would help us to socialize when we were older. George asked if it would help us to catch rabbits and kill rats and promptly got a smack round the ear. We were going to do sword dances and reels but we had to start off with a move called the Paddy Baa, which was a basic move for a lot of dances, or so she said. You had to put your feet together and jump up and down kicking your feet out like you were trying to get your socks off. It was hilarious at first and the girls seemed to do it better than the boys. George said he was going to the toilet and we never noticed he hadn't come back, until Mrs. Leven was looking for a partner for Peggy Rae. George didn't like Peggy Rae or dancing, so he had decided to hide.

It was time for the milk break and Mrs. Leven asked everyone to look for George and ask him to return but no one could find him. They looked everywhere bar up the top of the fir tree at the back of the toilets. When I went for a pee he was sitting in the old crow's nest at the top of the tree making signs to me to keep my mouth shut.

Anyway, it wasn't unusual for George to go missing for a while and nobody bothered too much and the class carried on. In the break Mrs. Leven had made up two wooden swords for the sword dance and we all took turns in doing the Paddy Baa and dancing round the swords while Mrs. Leven played the piano. It was quite good fun in the end and I think George missed out and knew it because I spied him kecking through the window looking a bit sheepish.

All that week we did a bit of dancing at school, as well as ordinary lessons. The next week Mrs. Leven said she was going to teach us how to knit.

Burning the heather

Come the weekend the Old Man decided he wanted to burn a couple of acres of heather because he wanted more grass on the hill and the heather was stifling the grass. As it had been dry and windy this week, the heather would burn easily and it had to be done before the Grouse started nesting. So he got Robert Cowan his mate from Torthorald who was visiting and Barnsey the herdsman to give a hand. They got a can of paraffin and made up torches with some old hessian sacks tied onto a couple of broken brush handles with a bit of barbed wire so they could drag the flaming torches through the heather.

Everything was ready, so off they went with old Nell the collie and Chips the terrier plus George and me tagging along behind. We thought there might be some rabbits in the heather to catch but more than that we wanted to see the fire and the heather burning. There was a bit of a breeze but it wasn't cold and you could see for miles.

When we got up to where they had to burn the heather, the men started pouring paraffin on the sacking and tried to light them, but the wind kept blowing the matches out. So they huddled round and made a wind break to shelter the sacking, so it would catch alight. Sure enough they soon got them going and started dragging them along the edge of the heather. Their touches were quite effective because with a long handle you could stop for a while set the heather alight but not get burnt. With two torches the heather soon got going.

George and me took the dogs and ran down to the far end to see if there were any rabbits scooting out of the heather. There were no rabbits but a couple of Grouse took flight when the dogs went into the heather sniffing about. They wouldn't be nesting yet, not in March. We started stamping about following the dogs and the fire was starting to take hold but all of a sudden the wind got up and changed direction a bit and the flames came racing towards us. We soon forgot about looking for rabbits and ran. Robert Cowan come out of the smoke shouting.

"You boys alright?"

"Yeah" We shouted, getting back up wind of the now roaring inferno. It only took about an hour for it to burn out. There were no rabbits but it was good fun and we certainly had learnt what could happen if you played with fire.

The men decided to walk back home past the old Roman fort so they could check on the old Galloway cows that had been put out earlier in the week and make sure they were ok and had plenty of food.

As we passed underneath the hill with the old fort on it, there was a bog about the same size as the patch of heather we had just burnt and when you walked on it, it wobbled like a jelly. In the middle was an open pool of water - not very big, about the size of a double bed or the back kitchen table. Robert Cowan reckoned that when the Romans were there, they used to tie a boulder to the prisoner's legs and just shove them in and you would never see them again.

"Aye." Dad said. "You would never see them again, a terrible way to go." Barnsey said, last year he was up here with the tractor and had a 56 lb weight in the trailer with a roll of twine. He tied the weight to the twine and threw it in the middle of the pool and the whole lot just disappeared.

"That was an awful lot of binder twine." Robert Cowan said it must be bottomless.

"Aye and full of skeletons and all swimming about down there." Dad said. Barnsey then dived on George, got some twine out of his pocket and started to tie his legs together. Robert Cowan said,

"I'll just get a big boulder." George was screaming. Barnsey said.

"This is what we do to naughty boys when we get the chance. Nobody will ever know. We're all sworn to secrecy." I ran and ran, hardly taking a breath and not looking back, all the way down the hill like I had wings on my feet. I didn't stop and went flying into the back kitchen past Mum and Aunty May and hid under the wireless screaming

"They've killed George, They've killed George." Mum and Aunty May were going mad when I told them what the men had done to George. I was just finishing off when Aunty May shouted

"Here's the men coming down the hill and George is with them." The dogs came running in the kitchen and found me quivering under wireless and George was alright. It was all a big joke. I had run away so fast they couldn't tell me. But to this day, I don't like secret societies. George said it scared him too. He said Barnsey was winking at him, so he knew he was alright and then he called me a scaredy cat for running away.

17

After that we used to give the bog under the old fort a wide berth, especially in the fog.

The smell of spring

George stayed with us that weekend but that wasn't unusual he more or less stayed every weekend and many weekdays too. So Monday morning it was off to school. It was a mile down the road and the end of winter was nigh. The smell of spring was in the air and there was a little spring in our steps too as we looked for crows pairing up and building their nests. You could sense something was going to happen. Yes springtime was round the corner and the longer days were coming and we would have more time to go bird nesting and rabbiting. We were full of the joys of spring, although it wasn't here yet.

But you could definitely smell it.

One plain one purl

On arriving at school Mrs. Leven was there as usual, ringing her bell and ushering us through the door. It was the first time this year she hadn't put a log fire on. But that wasn't surprising, because it was a great day. We got settled at our desks and after roll call we started on our times tables and alphabets.

Mrs. Leven got a box of knitting needles and a bagful of wool wrapped up in balls. She then announced. "After the break boys and girls, we're going to start learning how to knit and darn, so you'll be able darn your socks and mend the elbows on your jumpers and save your Mum a lot of work." George asked if it would help us to socialize when we were older and promptly got a clip behind the ear from his Mum – the teacher saying,

"It might not help you George but it would certainly help me."

After the break Mrs. Leven showed us how to do the knitting. We all gathered around her desk and she sat down getting out a couple of knitting needles and a ball of wool.

"This is how you do it children." She said. "First you cast on like this, then you do one plain one purl, one plain one purl and so on and with lots of practice, one day you could end up with a woolly jumper."

George looked at me and I looked at George and at that moment we knew we would never knit a woolly jumper. If we wanted a woolly jumper we would have to buy one. Or maybe get Aunty May to knit one. Then I remembered Aunty May knitted me a pair of socks with reclaimed wool for Christmas. They were that big I could put them on over my wellies, with room to spare. I had to give them to Barnsey the herdsman and they were nearly too big for him and he's nearly twenty. No. If I want a woolly jumper, I'll definitely buy one.

We all had a go and the girls were much better than the boys. I think they had been practicing at home with their Mums. George and me preferred rabbiting, ratting and birds nesting. We'll leave the knitting to the girls.

Lambing

When we got back from school, the Old Man had set up the paddock ready for the lambing to start. He had built shelters with bales of straw and partitioned a couple of loose boxes off for the weaker lambs and ewes that had to be kept in the warm. Lambing would start any day now and go on for a couple of weeks but Dad was ready. We had the Easter holiday's coming and we could give a hand.

Sure enough at the weekend the first lambs were born. Two sets of twins and one single. The weather was holding good and everybody was busy. Dad was doing the lambing, Barnsey was doing the milking and cultivating the fields that had been ploughed up in the autumn ready to sow the spring corn and plant the spuds. Sandy Carson was coming back from Canada to stay with us and lend a hand and Johnny the painter was back for Easter after having the winter off. Things were buzzing and the days were getting longer. Things were looking good for George and me.

The lambing got into full swing and there were ewes and lambs everywhere. Dad was working himself to death. He

19

didn't stop until nearly midnight and was up again at five. He put the ewes that he thought would lamb first in the barn so he could catch them easily. Quite often we would go with him to hold the Tilley lamp and give him a hand carrying the lambs. Sometimes one would die or be dead at birth and he would skin it there and then, take a lamb from a set of triplets and cover the live lamb with the skin of the dead one, sewing it on with a bit of binder twine so it wouldn't fall off till the mother ewe got used to her adopted baby. We used to stand there for a minute or two and make sure they bonded. The Old Man said that if you don't rub afterbirth on and put the dead lamb's skin on the new lamb and if it didn't smell like her lamb the old ewe would kill it. She would stamp on it and butt it till it was dead. It always pays to keep an eye on them for a minute or two. Just in case. It's usually ok if she lets it suckle.

Dad commandeered the Rayburn when the lambing was in full swing. He could have two or three lambs lying on old sacks in front of the open oven doors to get the heat, the Old Man blowing in their mouths and sometimes giving them the kiss of life, rubbing their backs trying to get them back to life. But as soon as the lambs were back on their feet they were put back with their mothers.

Mum and Aunty May would be working around all this, doing the cooking. Needless to say mutton was off the menu for a couple of weeks.

Sowing corn and planting spuds

Next year we would have electricity. They already had it in Shieldhill and they had started putting up the electric poles to the outlying farms and by October we should be connected.

Barnsey had cultivated all the fields that had been ploughed in the autumn and was getting them ready for sowing and planting. He was going to dribble the spring corn in next week and on Saturday we were to plant the spuds. Sandy Carson had ridged the potato drills with old Meg, one of the Clydesdale horses, saying,

"The drills are that straight you could shoot a bullet down them." The Old Man had put bags of seed potatoes down the bottom of the field, about three or four drills apart, ready for planting. We made aprons out of Hessian sacks and we were all ready.

Saturday morning was here, it was all hands on deck. There was George and me, Barnsey, Sandy and Robert Cowan my Dad's mate from Torthorald, Brother John and even Mum. I'm sure the Old Man would have had the dogs planting tatties if he could. Mum had left Aunty May doing the tea and we were having dinner late.

"All hands to the grindstone" Aunty May said.

"Many hands make easy work" Dad said.

We got down to the field and tied our apron sacks on, filled the pouches with seed tatties and got going. We had to plant the spuds about a foot apart and it didn't half make your back ache bending down dibbling spuds. At dinner time Mum went back to the house to get a basket of sandwiches and big enamel can full of tea. So we didn't have to walk back to the farm and we could keep planting tatties.

When she got back, we all sat around on the sacks of spuds eating our grub, drinking our tea and having a chat. A bit like a picnic. After twenty minutes it was back to work. Sandy got old Meg hitched onto the ridger and started covering and ridging the spuds we had just planted. George and me wanted to have a go ridging, but Dad said we had to finish the planting first and let Sandy get on with his work. Then you can have a go.

"The faster you work, the sooner you can have a go." He said. After a while the end was in sight and George and me had to collect up all the empty sacks and bag them ready to take home before we could have a go with the horse. Sandy was coming down the field towards us but we had to wait till he had turned the horse round for our go. George went first, with Sandy standing closely behind, in case he couldn't cope with hanging on to the reins and the ridger. He did alright but it was a lot harder than he expected. I think Sandy was controlling it really. I thought,

"Old Meg had more control over Old Meg than George did." Now it was my turn. It was really hard and you couldn't relax for a moment or it would veer off to one side or the other. It would definitely have helped if we were twice as heavy and twenty times stronger. After a few minutes we had got our wish and once we had done it, we weren't all that interested anymore and we left Sandy alone to finish off his job in peace.

We started to walk back to the barn taking all the empty sacks with us and putting them in the dry.

After a while Sandy came back to the yard with Old Meg and put her in the stable before taking her harness and collar off and hanging them up. He then gave her oats and hay and brushed her down.

The Old Man went back to his sheep. Barnsey did the milking. Robert Cowan went back home to Torthorald. Mum and Aunty May did the dinner. All in all it had been a good day and everything that had to be done was done.

The weather was getting better all the time now. Spring was definitely on its way and the crows were starting to nest in the wood behind the Steadings. We started repairing our tree hut as we hadn't used it since the autumn.

Dad had got a grant to build a new Byre and Dairy for when the electricity came. And we got a brand new tractor. A wee grey Ferguson - Fergie. We had to be self-sufficient and not rely on foreign imports for food and stuff like we did in the war.

"Aye we must be self-sufficient." Dad said.

Illness

On Monday I couldn't go to school because I had a temperature. It was 101 deg. F and I had to stay in bed with my clay piggy hot water bottle. No school, no birds nesting, no ratting, no nothing till I got better. Mum was running around with an old doctor's book trying to find out what deadly disease may have befallen the family. George was not allowed near in case he got contaminated and spread whatever I had around the school. So he had to play at Shieldhill with Graeme Kirkpatrick.

It was good at first just lying in bed but after a while it got boring. The Doctor had said to Mum.

"Keep the boy in bed till the fever subsides and let him sweat it out for a couple of days." Sure enough after a couple of days I started to feel better and had got fed up with lying in bed. My bedroom had a small step down into it and a ledge and brace door with a snick latch to shut it. There were loose floor boards that creaked whenever anybody walked down the landing. The door was painted a dull brown colour but it did match the skirting boards and picture rails. There was a small window that looked out at the wood at the back of the Steadings and on the floor was the obligatory square of lino. Where it didn't fit the boards were painted black. The bed was springy with a clay piggy hot water bottle and chantey pot half under it.

On the wall there was an oil painting of a Highland Cow, standing in the Highlands. Where else would it be. It looked right messed up. I used to lie in bed and look at that picture every day, especially when I was ill. So I shot it with my little pellet gun. I shot it through the head. I shot it through the horns I shot it in the legs. I shot it everywhere. My Mum went mad because it was her sister, Aunty Ena who had painted it. At the time she wasn't my favorite aunt, because on holiday at her place the year before, she wouldn't let me eat anything until I had finished off my lentil soup. I hated lentil soup. I shot a lot of things in my room before I got a good hiding from my Dad.

When I think of all the things I've done
When young and daft and full of fun
It's no wonder folks were wary
Because I was kind of contrary
If mischief there was to be
All they had to do was look for me
I had this uncanny knack
To do things just for the crack
But when I shot the Highland Cow
I over stepped the mark somehow
My folks didn't see the funny side
I think my Aunty Ena cried.

A bird in the bush

As I was feeling better, it was back to school on Monday. After school finished we ran back home, straight into the back kitchen, past Aunty May and Mum and grabbed a big jam sandwich and a glass of milk, before going for miles and miles birds nesting and rabbiting. We covered everything for miles. No stone was left unturned and we were always interested in any new information especially on new or rare birds so we could add an egg to our collection. That's where Johnny the painter comes into it. He used to catch the train from Dumfries to Shieldhill every day when he was working on the farm and walk up from the station to the farm. He would sit with Barnsey in the back kitchen having a cup of tea before Barnsey did the milking and they were always joking and mucking about and used to tell us where to find bird nests and rabbits and rats.

"Well it so happens." Johnny said. "That walking up from the station the other day he had seen these two really rare birds. We were all ears. He said he was just passing the road down to Connell's farm when he spotted a rare bird called a Rusted Wire Pecker which he thought must be nesting near there in one of the fence posts or maybe a gate post nearby. And also, a few days earlier, he had seen a really rare duck. That was called A Whistling Tree Duck and it nested up trees. Remembering that priceless information we were on the lookout that day for these rarities. We got the bird book out but we couldn't find them in it. But that wasn't surprising, they were very rare. Johnny had said so.

We scoured every fence post for miles, but differed in our views about the size of the bird. George thought it was the same as a Blackbird. I thought it was more like a Wren. So George was checking gate posts and large straining posts and I was on ordinary fence posts. We spent all of our evenings that week looking for The Rusted Wire Pecker but didn't find one. We thought we spotted one but weren't close enough to be sure.

So at the weekend we decided to look for the Duck. About three-quarters of a mile from the farm there was a small burn called Spring Burn that bordered on to Ronnie Shuttleworth's farm - Bruntshields. We decided to look there. The trees on the banks were mainly silver birch and the odd oak. We searched up the trees, in the hedges and on the banks of the burn but didn't find anything. So we sat down by one of the deep pools on a fallen tree root to have a rest and a bit of think on what to do next. We sat there just whiling the time away, throwing twigs and bits of bark into the pool, watching them swirl around in the eddies before going on their way over the rocks and down the burn. The crows were cawing up in the trees and sparrows and finches were chirping away. A skylark was singing its heart out. But we couldn't hear any ducks quacking. We decided to go up the boundary of a field called the Leys, which had a few trees and a ditch that led down to the burn. It was also on the way home. We started to check the trees as we passed them and had done three or four with no luck and were beginning to lose interest when George spotted a large hole in the next one. We climbed up and were flabbergasted to find a ducks nest. It was about ten feet up and there were eight eggs. This had to be it. A Whistling Tree Duck. A very rare bird. There were two eggs just about to hatch, so we got back down the tree and went fifty yards into the hayfield and lay in the grass to see what would happen. Sure enough after a few minutes there was a lot of fluttering and the mother came back. George and me were really excited, we both thought The Whistling Tree Duck looked a bit like a Mallard but then all female birds look a bit dull in plumage.

We couldn't wait to get back to tell everybody the news, especially Johnny the painter. But it was the weekend and Johnny wasn't working and we wouldn't be able to tell him until after school on Monday. We couldn't wait to see the look on his face when we told him. It rained like mad the next day, so we didn't go near the nest.

On Monday after school we ran home to catch Johnny and tell him. He was gob smacked. We felt like heroes as we walked down the Leys to show him. When we got to the tree, we let Johnny climb up first and stood back to watch. We thought he was joking when he said there was nothing in the nest but when we climbed up, sure enough it was empty, just a couple of shells. One was two thirds whole, so we gathered it up to put in our egg collection. Johnny then pointed out to us what had happened. When ducklings hatch they leave the nest more or less straight away and head for the nearest water, so as we had found the nest on Saturday and they were beginning to hatch. As this was Monday afternoon, they were well gone. We took the shell that was two thirds whole back with us for our collection. It was only two thirds whole, but it sat there, all wrapped up in cotton wool.

Looked real good. Pride of place in the box. A Whistling Tree Duck. A very rare egg indeed. We never did find the Rusted Wire Pecker.

The Hill in summer

Come the weekend George and me decided to go rabbiting over the back of the hill. We got our sticks and we took Old Nell the Collie and Chips the terrier with us. It was our first trip over the back of the hill this year. It was great to get up there and it was a great day as well. The bracken and heather were getting taller now and the dogs were disappearing down the rabbit runs. We could hear them yelping from time to time and sometimes they would come into view on an open track panting with their tongues hanging out and shaking the burrs off. They would give you a quick look before going straight up another run yelping away. They were loving it and so were we. It was great to be up the hill on a nice day rabbiting with George and the dogs.

Old Nell finally caught one. I took it off her and held it up by its back legs and George whacked it with his stick. We had no sooner done that, when Old Nell caught another. We dispatched it the same way and started up over the hill heading for home. After twenty minutes we reached the top of the high North hill and just sat there. Resting and admiring the view.

We had been on the go for two or three hours and our journey had taken up right up the back of the hill looking for birds' nests and trying to catch the odd rabbit. We had just got the two. This was our favorite resting spot when up the hill and on route for home. But it was so hot.

"We'll paunch these rabbits here." George said.

"OK might as well." I replied, handing him my pocket knife. George got one of the rabbits, cut its guts open, cleaned it out and stuck one of its back legs with the knife and knitted the other leg through, ready to carry on our sticks. Then he did the other one, complaining about the flies as he threw the guts away from us.

"They'll go after the guts and give us a break." he said, swatting flies with a swathe of grass. "Bloody flies." We settled down again and just lay there in the sun, chewing on the stems of grass. The hill, to us, was like the sea to a sailor. It had a calling. It was always a great feeling to be up the hill, walk through the bracken and heather in the early summer, see rabbits scoot down their holes, and hear whaps and pewits and see larks hovering way up in the sky, singing their hearts out.

"It's no like this in winter." George said.

"No, you can say that again." I replied, remembering how harsh it was when we came rabbiting in the winter with snowdrifts and pawmarks, peemarks and droppings in the snow. And your breath going up in big clouds of steam in the cold air, taking the skin off your lips and you would be crying in pain with the cold in your fingers. You would flap your arms and stamp your feet so hard you would nearly take off.

We looked across to Queensbury and noticed a sort of darkness in the sky. The birds had stopped singing and even the flies didn't seem so active. So we decided to make for home and started ambling down the hill with our rabbits hanging on our sticks slung over our shoulders. The dogs tagged along jumping up every now and then sniffing at the rabbits and sometimes grabbing them.

We had only gone a few yards, when the biggest flash of lightning and the loudest bang of thunder we'd ever heard, happened. It seemed right next to us. Fear hit us. Complete panic. The dogs were gone in the blink of an eye and we weren't far behind them. The rabbits and sticks were abandoned and we ran so fast down the hill we nearly caught the dogs up. We were falling over and rolling. We were taking no chances. We just kept going driven on by fear. The Devil himself wouldn't have caught us. The cobbled yard and back kitchen door was the objective. As fast as possible. Every man for himself. Grandpa and Aunty May had been looking out for us when they heard the thunder. They knew we wouldn't be long. We flew in the back kitchen door and I hid under the wireless behind Grandpa's chair and George went under the kitchen table.

Grandpa lit up his pipe and Aunty May put the kettle on to make a cup of tea, humming a little tune as she did so. The workers started to wander in out of the rain to have a cup of tea and were sitting round the table chatting and having a fag. Me and George came out of our hiding places and things soon began to calm down. The old folks didn't seem to worry too much about the thunder but I suppose they had seen it all before. Old Sandy Carson said.

"A few years ago when he was fencing, there was a storm and he took shelter under a tree from the rain. When the rain stopped he went back to his fencing and was working away, when a bolt of lightning hit the tree he had been standing under just a few minutes earlier. "

"You could feel the shock come up the wire that I was holding he said and I was a hundred yards away with my rubber wellies on. Aye, nature's a powerful thing." God knows what would have happened If I had put my tackity boots on that morning. "Doesn't bare thinking about," he murmured. Soon the sun was shining again and everybody went back to their work. George and me decided we would leave the sticks and rabbits where they were for now and maybe pick them up another day. We weren't going back up there. Not for a while at least. That had scared the life out of us and the dogs as well.

Smoking chaff

The weather got worse later in the week. It rained for a couple of days and we couldn't find much to do after school. Robert and Austin Telfer from the next door farm had walked back with us from school and we were playing in the barn. We were climbing up onto a big wooden beam and dropping into a heap of straw, just like a paratrooper, when George decided to climb onto another beam and dive into the chaff piled up at the end of the barn. He disappeared, just like he had dived into water. We were all flabbergasted and stood there waiting for

George to reappear out of the chaff. There was a silent pause followed by an eruption of chaff. George emerged like some kind of monster spitting out chaff and sneezing.

We all fell about laughing and made such a noise that my brother John and his mate David Marshal from Barshill far heard the commotion and came running in to see what was going on. When they saw the state that George was in, they gave us a hand to clean him up and make him look half respectable.

When we finished, we sat around having a chat and messing about wondering what to do next, when somebody wondered what it would be like to smoke chaff.

"It must be much the same as smoking tobacco." Austin said.

"Grandpa's old pipes are in a jar on the mantle shelf in the back kitchen." Brother John chirped in. Davy said.

"But how are you going to get past your Mum and your Aunty May and get the pipes. They're always in the back kitchen." They then left. So we would have to get a pipe ourselves. We had to devise a cunning plan. We decided that George, Robert and Austen, would go round the front of the house and Rob and Austen would beat up George. So he would make such a noise and commotion in the front porch that Mum and Aunty May would leave the back kitchen and come to the front door to see what all the noise was about. I would then sneak in the back kitchen and nick a pipe. It was all set to go, everybody was in place. So I gave the whistled signal we had arranged. Sure enough I could hear the commotion from the back of the house. Aunty May and Mum went rushing to the front door. To see what was happening. I rushed in the back door, stood on a chair and grabbed two pipes and a box of matches and legged it.

We mustered back in the chaff barn. It had been a perfect mission. We stood there by the big heap of chaff, sucking on the pipes, to sort of get the hang of it. Brother John and Davy came in and seeing we had got the pipes, took them of us, saying we were too young to be smoking and they were going to try them out first. We didn't mind because the empty pipes had left a horrible taste in our mouths. Unbeknown to us, Dad had come home from the market and was having a cup of tea.

Mum and Aunty May said they thought we boys were up to something because we were acting a bit funny and fighting.

"I'm sure something's afoot" Mum said. Back in the barn, John and Davy were stuffing the pipes full of chaff to have a go at smoking. All they needed was a match and I had the matches and I was on top of the beam above the straw. They started to hit me with the yard brush and threw cow cake at me, till I finally fell off into the straw and their arms and they soon had the matches off me. Things calmed down and John and Davy were trying to light their pipes, sucking like mad, coughing and looking a sickly white, with tears in their eyes. We were just standing around watching them.

That's when we noticed the Old Man standing at the barn door with his shepherds crook. When I say we saw him, I meant, George, me, Bob and Austen. But not Davy and Brother John. They were too preoccupied with their pipes. Also nobody had heard the Old Man coming, because he had bought a new pair of boots at the market and they had rubber soles and he had sneaked up on us with no warning, just like a cat. A big ugly cat with a big nobly stick, that wasn't too happy to see matches being lit in amongst the chaff and straw. George and me and the Telfer boy's legged it. Unfortunately Brother John and Davey weren't aware of their impending doom. With their watery eyes and sickly looks, cornered down the end of the barn, things didn't look to good for them. We could hear them taking a fair old beating.

"At least if he kicks them, it shouldn't hurt too much, with his new rubber soles." George said.

"If he had been wearing his tackity boots we would have heard him walking on the cobbles in the yard" I chipped in, as we headed for the safety of our tree hut.

John and Davy were very unlucky. Very unlucky indeed. I think it put them off smoking for life. Robert and Austen didn't come to play for ages after that.

The scales of justice

On Monday morning the builders come from Lochmaben to start on the foundations of the new byre and dairy. Dad had got a grant and it had to be built ready for when we got the electricity in the autumn. George and me wanted to stay and help but Mum and Aunty May told us to get off on down the road to school. We really wanted to stay but Mum was adamant.

When we got back from school, the builders had set the outline of the byre and dairy out with twine tied to iron pegs and they had already started the digging. There were heaps of sand and bags of cement stacked up in the barn. There was also a concrete mixer with a petrol engine and planks and ladders and trestles. There were all sorts of things for us to play with. We couldn't wait for the weekend.

The weekend soon came around and Robert and Austin Telfer came over to play and go birds nesting. Later on Bob Wilson came over from Lockerby to stay for the weekend. We all went round to see how the new byre was getting on. There was some planks lying on the ground and we put one of them on a trestle and started using it as a see saw. It was great fun and everybody wanted a go.

Then we got a bigger trestle to make it go higher but the plank was too short and it wouldn't work. We were just about to give up on it, when Austin suggested we should use a ladder instead of a plank, because it was at least twice as long. Everybody thought that was a great idea. It was soon lugged out of the barn and we put it on the biggest trestle we could find. It went really high into the air but it slipped on the trestle, so Austin tied the middle rung of the ladder with a rope to stop it slipping and we were ready to go. There was only one problem. How to get onto it.

We decided the Telfer boy's would sit on one side of the see saw and Bob and me would go on the other side, because we were a similar weight. George would have to miss all the fun, because he was too light. When the Telfer boys sat on their end of the ladder, our end was about ten foot in the air and we couldn't figure out how to get on it. But there had to be a way. If Dad had a problem, he would say.

"Where there's a will, there's a way."

We tried climbing up the rungs of the ladder but it kept wobbling and we fell off before we could get to the end of it.

The Telfer's were sitting on their end of the ladder waiting for us to sort ourselves out and get some action.

There was a tree branch just above our end of the ladder and we decided to climb up the tree and along the branch, then we could lower ourselves down onto the ladder and start see sawing. George followed along the branch behind us saying that he wanted to have a go too. Bob lowered himself down onto the end of the ladder and got comfortable and then I dropped down on the rung in front of him and let go of the branch but nothing happened. Robert and Austin were too heavy. They tried pushing up with their feet but it wasn't quite enough. We were too light. There had to be an answer. We had the will all we needed was the way. The answer was there, right above us. Sitting on the branch. The answer was George. If he jumped on as well we would have the extra weight and we would be able to get on with our see sawing. George was all for it and scrambled along the branch and hung down and put his feet on the ladder ready to let go.

The Telfor's gave us the nod and George let go. Problem was there was a George of a difference in the weight and we really only needed a quarter of a George. We plummeted earthwards while the Telfer's shot skywards. On hitting the ground Bob and me fell off, the Telfer's zoomed earthwards and George was doing acrobatics just as if he was in the circus. The Telfer's hit the ground with a thud and were running around holding there arses going,

"Ooh Ah," and shouting "Jesus Christ." George flew through the air doing summersaults but landed in the midden. He always was a lucky boy.

The mixer

After all the excitement with the see saw, nobody wanted to try it out again and it was getting hot. George was washing some of the muck off after his acrobatic trip into the midden. He was using the water butt next to the cement mixer that the builders used to build the new byre and dairy.

The mixer had a small petrol engine. Robert and Austin thought they knew how to start engines. That seemed interesting and we wanted to know more and to see if we could do it. Austin said they start it with a short bit of rope with a knot in it, wrapped around that spindle with the hook on it. We found the rope tied to the framework of the cement mixer.

Austin seemed to know what he was doing so we all stood back and watched full of anticipation. He switched the petrol on and wrapped the rope around the spindle thing and grabbed hold of the wooden toggle on the end of the rope, and pulled like hell but to no avail. After two or three attempts, Austin was about to give up but encouraged by our enthusiasm and never say die attitude, he carried on but soon had to give up. That didn't matter because there were plenty of us there that could pull. So no problem.

Austin was not about to be beaten and started to analyze the situation. Starting with the petrol. He pulled the on off valve in and out and checked that the tank had petrol in it. That was OK. It was then that Robert remembered that when they had a cement mixer at their farm a year ago, they used to stop it working by pressing something on the top of the engine. I think it was that springy thing on top of the plug, "Yea" he said, "that springy metal thing on top of the plug"

We all gathered round and Austin fiddled with the bit of springy metal on top of the plug and sure enough when he twisted it to the side it came off. On seeing that, there was a new fervor in the atmosphere and Austin wrapped the rope around the spindle, grabbed the wooden toggle and he pulled the engine over. It only gave a slight splutter and didn't fire up but it gave everybody a little hope and, after a couple of pulls, it started, with lots of smoke and noise and all us shouting and squealing and watching it go round and round. As the smoke gradually disappeared we put the empty mixer in the three different positions, fill, mix and empty.

After a few minutes it got a bit boring and somebody wondered what it might be like to sit in the barrel while it was going round. Everybody thought that was a good idea and we asked for a volunteer. No one stepped forward, so we decided to pick one and it was unanimously decided that George should be selected. Well it wasn't quite unanimous because there was one vote against but that was George. His vote didn't count, because he was the winner.

Austin put the springy bit of metal on the top of the plug and sure enough, everything stopped. George was quite keen to get in and we helped him get into the mixer, which was in the upright fill position. We shouted,

"Are you all right," and he gave us cheery thumbs up. All he needed was a red scarf and a leather helmet and he would have looked like Biggles, or maybe The Red Baron.

Austin wrapped the rope around the spindle and pulled like hell. The engine started first pull and the barrel was rotating smoothly with George seemingly enjoying himself. We then decided to put George in the mix mode. This was a lot better for us to see him as we could look straight in the barrel. It made us dizzy watching him going round and round. It was time to get George out of the mixer but maybe we should have turned the engine off before we put the mixer in the empty mode but George wouldn't drop out.

Finally, Austin switched the engine off. There was a silence, a very silent silence, and then George slipped out of the mixer and onto the spot board, just like a calf being born.

The fly catchers

After all the excitement with the see saw and cement mixer, nobody wanted to try it out again and it was getting to hot. We started looking for birds' nests in the spinney behind the farm buildings. We climbed up to the rooks nest to see how many eggs they had in them.

Barnsey the herdsman said that if a crow builds a nest on the branch of a tree, it will be strong enough to take the weight of a man. We were only boys, so we should be alright.

George was swinging on the rope hanging down from our tree hut. By God it was hot, bloody flies everywhere. We all gathered on the ground at the bottom of the tree, with our tree hut in it, swatting flies away. They were a real pest. George wanted a pee and because George wanted a pee everybody else wanted a pee. So we all got our willies out and stood round the bottom of the tree peeing.

All of sudden George shouted "I've got one, I've got one."
"You've got what." Austin said.

"I've got a fly trapped under my foreskin, like a flytrap."
George said, as we all looked on as he pulled his foreskin back
to show us.

As he did so the fly took flight and we all started laughing.
So we all decided to have a go. After all there were plenty of
flies about and we had nothing better to do. So we all
presented arms. Willies out. Foreskins back. Last one to catch
a fly is a sissy. We soon started catching them and they didn't
half tickle when you caught one.

Looking back on it that was probably the first time I had
ever had my fancy tickled. It was hilarious. Everybody was
laughing. Except Bob. Everybody stopped laughing and
looked at him. He hadn't caught any flies. On closer
inspection, we noticed he had something missing. He hadn't
got a foreskin.

"You can't catch flies in your foreskin, if you haven't got
one."

"Why in the name of the wee man, haven't you got a
foreskin?" Asked Austen. "Everybody else has.."

Bob looked really embarrassed and said.

"When I was very young I had something called a 'circus
situation' and they must have stolen my foreskin. I suppose
they did it to stop me catching flies when I got older."

Everybody nodded in agreement.

"Well." Austin said. "If he couldn't catch flies, he could see
which one of us caught the most flies."

George won and he nearly caught a bluebottle.

Barnsey had just started milking the cows and had sprayed
DDT right down the Byre to get rid of the flies and stop the
cows from swishing their tails and kicking. Sometimes he
would tie their tails back so he could milk them without getting
swished.

We stood and watched Barnsey for a minute and then got
hold of the fly spray. It was empty, so we got the gallon can of
DDT and filled it up for Barnsey and then started spraying one
another to keep the flies off. It really did work.

So we all stood there and got sprayed. We had fly spray running down our hair and our faces, into our eyes and mouths. Everywhere. We all turned a streaky yellow.

After that, there were no FLIES on US.

The sheep shite fight

We were walking back from an unsuccessful Rabbit hunt. There was just the four of us, George, Graham Kirkpatrick, Bob Wilson and me and we were all getting a bit bored.

When we got to the Spring Burn, we sat on the bank throwing bits of bark from an old broken branch into the water and watched as they swirled downstream and in and out of the different eddies. That got boring too, so we started throwing stones at the floating bark for target practice. It was all right for a minute or two and then that got boring as well.

Starting for home, we headed up a field called the Leys, which was on the way home. We had called it a day. It was just one of those days when nothing seemed to go right.

"You can't have a good time all the time. Can you?" George said, kicking a bit of sheep shite. It went zinging up the field before finally flying into pieces.

"That was a good kick," someone said and George responded by kicking another one. That's when we noticed loads of sheep shite. It was everywhere so we decided to have a sheep shite fight but we had to have rules.

There was only one rule, agreed by everyone. No stones, just sheep shite.

It was George and me versus Bob and Graham.

It started off quite sedately at first. It wasn't too messy and if you kept your distance and your eye on the ball, or in this case sheep shite, you could avoid the worst of it.

But Bob made a big mistake. He was in no man's land, looking for better ammo. Big mistake. Because when he was bending down, sorting out the ammo, we all ganged up on him. We came out of the sun and attacked from everywhere. He was a sitting duck.

A severe Sheep shiteing took place. The hard stuff was for long distance, bombarding and rifling. The soft stuff was for close quarters and hand to hand fighting. Once we had finished with Bob, we all turned on each other. It was all out war. Complete mayhem.

After a few minutes, an uneasy truce was called. Nobody really won and we were all in a right mess. Maybe Bob was slightly worse. But we had a good laugh and it broke the tension. But now the hour of reckoning had arrived and we had to go home and face the music.

George and Grahame went straight back to Shieldhill bypassing the farm. But Bob and me had to go back to the farm, where his Mum was due to pick him up in about an hour with their brand new car.

We walked into the yard and up to the back kitchen door. Nell the old sheepdog lay there in the sun. Chips the terrier ran out on hearing us followed by Mum.

She took one look at us and immediately started to give me a really good slapping, saying,

"How could you get in such a mess, you silly buggers." Get in the bath right away, before Bob's mother comes to pick him up and for Christ's sake don't be so bloody daft. Ye just cause us a lot of work, cleaning and everything." Slapping us all the way to the bath.

I heard Aunty May say, "Silly boys, just cause us a lot of work. As if we haven't got enough to do."

Bob's mother arrived in her new car, A Triumph Mayflower with red leather seats. Smelt real nice. I love the smell of new things.

She wouldn't let Bob or me go near it and Mum had to give Bob a spare pair of pajamas and all his dirty gear was put in a brown paper bag and shoved in the boot. He had to sit on the back seat once they had put a blanket on it.

I think Bob was in for a real good slapping when he got back home. He looked petrified and was shaking. A condemned man.

Bob's Mum had a face like thunder, as they drove out of the back yard. Mum and Aunty May had lost their venom, out of slapping me. It had been a funny old day. Full of ups and downs. I had to go to bed early,

"Aye. Up the golden stairs boy, said Aunty May. "And if you canny get to sleep, just try counting sheep."

Ronnie's bogie

"Must take Ronnie's bogie trailer back." Dad said.

We had borrowed his bogie when our one had a puncture and we still had some hay to take to the barn. He looked at me.

"You could take it son. Take the wee grey Fergie and go down to Fernieclough on the road and across the fields at the back of the Leys and into Bruntshields through the back way."

I was really excited. 9 years old and I have to take Ronnie's bogie back. All the way to Bruntshields. A real responsible job. I backed the wee Fergie up to the bogie and hitched it on to the drawbar, making sure the pin was in and away I went down the road towards Fernieclough. The wee Fergie was purring away nicely when I reached Ronnie's gate at the back of the leys. I stopped, put the hand break on, got off and opened the gate and drove through into the field, shutting the gate after me.

There were loads of ruts, especially around the gates and it was really bumpy all the way down the track to Ronnie's.

When I finally arrived at Bruntshields, Ronnie was in the yard forking hay, so I drove up beside him and switched the engine off.

Ronnie greeted me with a cheery,

"Hello and what brings you here then."

"I've brought your bogie trailer back Ronnie," I said.

"Where have you put it then son." Ronnie enquired.

"It's on the back of the......" I stopped in mid-sentence. It wasn't on the back of the tractor. It was there at the gate opposite Fernieclough.

I looked at Ronnie for an answer.

"Don't worry son. It's probably bounced off in them ruts up the field a bit. Let's go and see."

He jumped on the drawbar of the tractor and we headed back up the field and sure enough there it was sitting amongst some bad ruts in a gateway. I reversed up to it and we hitched up. The hitch pin was lying there on the floor and this time Ronnie put a snap pin in it, to stop it from coming out.

Off we went and we were soon back in Ronnie's yard. I thanked Ronnie saying,

"Din 'aye tell me Old Man," and off I went."

On getting back to the gate at Ferniclough, I seen Robert and Austin Telfer walking up the road from the end of their drive and felt real important standing there wi' the wee Fergie ticking over.

"Just took the Bogie we borrowed back to Ronnie's for my Dad. On my own you know." Emphasizing, 'on my own you know.'

"We were just coming up to your place to go rabbiting, so you can give us a lift and save us walking." Rob said. They both clambered on standing on the drawbar and hanging onto the mudguards and off we went. Hightown soon loomed up and we drove into the cobbled yard, in front of the back kitchen.

Everybody was having a cup of tea and when I switched the engine off, I heard Barnsey say,

"He's back Tom. He's back"

Through the window I could see the Old Man put the phone down.

I think they had been watching out for me all the time in case I came to grief and the line from Ronnie's to Amesfield 282 had been buzzing. I had just completed my first dangerous mission.

I wondered if Ronnie had told my Dad about the Bogie.

Ooer Willy

We used to have lots of people visit the farm on a business basis. This usually turned into some sort of friendship. They always seemed to turn up just before dinner or teatime because everybody knew they would be asked to stay. There was always plenty to eat and usually enough for second helpings too. Mum always used to make extra just in case someone turned up unexpected. If nobody turned up that day she would make potato scones on the griddle and fry them up for breakfast the next morning.

One day Willy Hall who was working as a salesman for Bibby's, the stock feed merchants, turned up as usual to take his monthly order and get paid for last month's delivery of stock feed. Now Willy was a large man who for those days was well travelled. He always wore a tweed suit, brogue shoe's, a red spotted handkerchief in his lapel pocket, a nice tie or cravat and a trilby, usually with a couple of fly fishing hooks stuck in the side. Willy was the kind of man who could command respect with a look and voice of authority. To us anyway.

Well Willey used to like coming to the farm and, although he would come for dinner, he would quite often stay for tea as well. One day we were all sitting in the back kitchen having tea and chatting away, when my Dad said if we didn't get rain soon, all the crops would die. He said that you could get your hands down some of the cracks in the ground. It's that dry.

Willy nodded in agreement and said.

"Yes I know Tom. I've just been to the Hislop's at Glen Burn and he was saying the same. Oh by the way Tom, wee Jenny Hislop had a baby boy, on Monday."

"Is that so." Dad replied, pausing for a moment, "she's only been married for six weeks."

"Aye that's right." Willy said, "It must be the Atomic Age. Every thing's faster now."

Willy then started to go on about what nice plumbs and cherries we had in the wood. Well me and George looked at one and other in disbelief. We thought we knew every nook and cranny for miles around and we hadn't see any fruit in the wood, or anywhere else ether. So up we jumped and ran outside into the wood and started searching for the plumbs and cherries. We didn't have to search long before we found them. But they were really hard to get too, all the cherries were in what we thought was a cherry bush and the plumbs were in a hawthorn tree. We got scratched and prickled all over the place. I remember looking round and seeing my Dad and Willy through the kitchen window, roaring with laughter.

When we had picked enough, we climbed up into our tree hut to eat our booty.

"It's funny how things always seem to happen when Willy comes around." George said.

"Yeah." I muttered. "I wonder what an Atomic Age is."

"It must be about six weeks." George replied.

The cherry pickers

When Willy was about the farm.
He used to impress us with his charm.
And tell us of fruit up trees.
Blowing gently in the breeze.
And us, being young, daft and naive.
His aim, he would usually achieve.

A close clip

The time had come around to shear the sheep. The shearers
would be here on Monday morning, eight a.m. sharp. It was
Saturday morning and Dad was getting everything set up ready
for the men coming. George and me were going to give him a
hand. Everything had to be ready. Most of the sheep shearing
gear had been stored at the back of the coal shed. There were
four big wooden sheep shearing tripods, the shearer sat on the
small end and rolled the sheep so he could clip it without
kneeling and bending. This year was going to be different
though. Some of the men had got themselves these new-
fangled mechanical clippers and were on piece work and that
meant they got paid for each sheep they sheared and the old
boys with the hand clippers were on day work. So it should be
interesting to see who will win financially and there was going
to be a lot of rivalry, or so Dad said. Some of the old codgers
refused to move with the times and insisted on using the old
fashioned hand clippers. Dad had bought two sets of
mechanical clippers with a petrol engine which he bolted down
on the top of an old wooden bench at the back of the byre to
stop it shaking about.

The last thing we prepared was to string up a couple of
woolsacks in the barn ready for packing the fleeces in. When
we got about twenty in the bag, we stamped up and down on
them until Barnsey or somebody could sew the bag up with
binder twine. The sacks were all the same size and made of
really thick hessian and when you moved them when they were
full you used a sacking hook, because there was nowhere to

grab. There were always metal hooks hanging behind the barn door ready for this heavy work.

Come Sunday we got all the sheep off the hill and outlying fields and brought them down to the fields next to the paddock and pens, ready for catching on the Monday morning.

It was half term, so George and me had got a few days off school and we would be able to help catching sheep and packing the wool sacks and fetching tea and drinks for the men.

On the Monday we were all up at six to get some of the sheep in the pens ready for the catchers and then it was in for breakfast before the men started to arrive. Mum and Aunty May had lots to do today and lots of folks to feed and water.

"You can't work on an empty stomach." said Aunty May. "Get your breakfast down and you'll work twice as hard." So George and me had an extra egg and some more fried bread.

The workmen started arriving just before eight. Some were on tractors but one was on an old green ex-army motor bike with his collie sitting on the petrol tank in between his arms. Everyone had a good laugh when he swung into the yard. The men were from the neighbors' farms, like when we do the threshing. It's a sort of a communal thing. The catchers started catching the sheep and the old boys with the hand clippers started clipping and chatting away. Then the peace was broken. Two petrol engines should have been started but one wouldn't. The old boys were moaning like mad, shouting that the noise was terrible and you couldn't hear yourself think.

"By the time you get that other engine started, I could have sheared half a dozen sheep." One of them said. All the old boys gave a communal moan.

Eventually the other engine fired up and it was all go. A rhythm developed with hand shearers slow, mechanical shearers faster. Come teatime at half past ten we would find out who was fastest. So for the next hour or so the shearers were going hammer and tongs and everyone was pleased to see Mum come around the corner with a couple of enamel cans of tea, so they could stop and have a rest.

The old boys were getting beaten and when we counted the fleeces the mechanical clippers were over twice as fast, by twenty fleeces to eight. We've not settled it yet, old Andy said.

Give us a couple days and let us settle in. The tea tasted real good and everybody was glad of the rest, even although it was only ten minutes but that gave George and me time to clean up the loose wool and oil the new mechanical clippers, then it was back to work. They started the engines and started shearing like mad trying to outdo each other. This made it hard work for us stacking the wool bags and catching the sheep and we were glad come dinner time, to have a break.

The men had got there packed lunches and Mum came out with cans of tea and freshly cooked buttered scones and we all sat down in the shade of the old tree at the back of the byre enjoying our lunch and all the banter that goes with it. George and me joined in with about five hundred sheep all bleating and baaing. I suppose they were having a chat as well while the petrol engines were switched off. But the lunch break was soon over, half an hour and off we went. Petrol engines on and it was blood, sweat and shears.

It took the best part of a week to finish the shearing and in the end the old boys had to reluctantly concede defeat. Next year it would be all piece work and mechanical clippers. That was the end of the shearing for this year.

Hay time

It was time to cut the hay. Sandy Carson was getting the reaper out of the barn to give it the once over, ready for mowing the hay. He was pouring old tractor oil all over any part that moved and greasing every grease nipple he could find. The reaper used to be pulled by old Meg the Clydesdale Shire but now it had been converted to be pulled by the wee grey Fergie. The mower still had the springy seat where you sat to control the horse but they didn't take it off because it wasn't in the way of anything. George and me could ride on it instead of walking behind when catching rabbits.

All Sandy had to do now was sharpen the blades that were hanging up in the barn. That would take a while because there was twenty blades on each shaft and some of them were broken. When they finished mowing last year, they just took out the shafts and hung them on the wall, saying they would repair and sharpen them in the winter. Winter came and went and now hay time was upon us. It was all happening and the reaper blades were still hanging on the wall where they had been hung up after mowing last year. Sandy took the blades and stood gripped the shaft in the vice on the bench. He started filing the blades sharp and when he got to the broken ones which were riveted onto the shaft, he filed the heads off the old rivets, knocked them through with a punch, replaced the old blades with new ones, and riveted them tight on the old anvil with the riveting hammer.

George come into the yard followed by old Nell and Chips the two dogs and came over to the barn where Sandy was getting the mower ready.

"All right George." said Sandy from underneath the mower where he was trying to insert the blades ready for mowing. Looking at the seat on the back of the mower George said,

"You'll not need the seat on the back of the mower now, 'cause you'll be sitting on the wee Fergie's tractor seat from now on. So we can sit on it and wait for the rabbits to bolt and save our legs."

"Aye that's right George and I'll no need to feed it or brush it down when I finish work either. I'll just pull the stop on the engine and that's that."

Sandy then said he was going to try it out in the paddock and cut the thistles and nettles there and make sure it's working ok, before he started cutting the hay on Monday. He then lifted up the reaper blade so he could drive it through the gate and George me and the two dogs followed him into the paddock to see how it all worked.

He let the blade down, giving it a quick kick with his hob-nailed boots, before jumping back onto the tractor and starting to mow the thistles and nettles in the paddock. We got our sticks and ran behind the mower with the two dogs, just in case there were any rabbits clumped down in the tufts of grass and nettles. It was hard work trying to keep up and George grabbed the seat on the back of the mower and jumped on. I tried to get on but kept falling off and Sandy wouldn't stop and I'm sure George didn't make it easy for me anyway.

Sandy was just about to finish and I was getting a bit tired of running behind the mower when it cut through a partridge's nest with the mother partridge sitting on it. Sandy stopped and old Nell grabbed the mother Partridge but she had both her legs cut off and had a broken wing, so Sandy put her out of her misery by smacking her head on the metal wheel of the mower. We looked at the nest, some of the eggs were broken and they would have hatched out in a day or two.

"That's the way it goes boys, another couple of days and they would have been hatched and gone and then we would have probably shot most of them in the winter in the shooting season. I would have stopped if had seen her but they sit so tight and they're so well camouflaged I didn't see a thing."

As he went to get back on the tractor he put his boot on the nest and broke all the eggs, murmuring,

"That's the way it goes, I just didn't see her." He then carried on mowing and finished off cutting the paddock.

We took the partridge back into the barn and thought about giving it a proper burial but decided to give it to the ferrets instead. They went crazy when they smelled the warm blood. We sat and watched for a minute or two, until things settled down.

Mum shouted us in for dinner and all of the afternoon's traumas were soon forgotten. But as Sandy says,

"That's the way it goes."

Chariots of fire

Old Meg was used sparingly once we got the little grey Fergie tractor. She was made more or less redundant and only used on wet ground or light work like on wet ground which the tractor couldn't get to and for jobs like ridging potato drills and raking hay which was loose in the field. We would rake it into lines so that the hay sweep could gather it in ready to put on the tripods to dry.

Well one day I was helping to get the hay in and Dad hitched old Meg onto the hay rake which was about 15 foot wide with long tines about 4 inches apart and a lever that you pulled when you wanted to release the hay which was left in a row. This all worked from a ratchet cog on the wheels. There was a large springy metal seat that stuck out the back with a foot rest.

Anyway Dad said he wanted me to do the work so he set everything up and we had a trial run. He sat on the seat and I ran alongside watching what to do. After a while I couldn't keep up with him and my wellies had left big red rings around my legs where they had rubbed. Dad went up and down a couple of times to give me an idea of what to do then he stopped next to me. I got on the seat and then he handed me the reigns. I couldn't quite reach the footrest unless I sat sideways, though. Well I gave the horse the "giddee up" but nothing happened so Dad gave old Meg a slap on the rear and off we went.

We went up and down for about half an hour and I was getting quite used to it and it started getting a bit boring so I tried to get old Meg to go a little faster but she wouldn't have any of it. Then I remembered if you made a farting noise she would bolt, so I blew a raspberry. Well it went from a gentle stroll to what seemed like full gallop in seconds. I got such a shock I didn't know what to do. I was pulling on the reigns and shouting "whoa" but with my feet unable to reach the footrest I had no power to pull on the reins it was like charging around on a chariot, so I abandoned ship.

I remember lying on the ground looking at the rear end of the horse galloping towards the ten foot gate, with the fifteen foot rake, heading towards the stable. Well thank god it slowed down a bit before it hit the gate and it didn't do too much damage. My Dad and grandpa didn't worry about me as they ran past to get the horse. I think I heard something about a bloody stupid boy and I needed a good kick up the arse but they were in too much of a hurry to stop and I escaped a spanking.

By the time they untangled the horse, the rake and the gate, I was nowhere to be found.

The whittler

Bob Wilson's mother, Mrs. Tweedy, used to drop Bob off to stay at the farm for the odd weekend during the year, especially in the summer when we could play longer in the light nights, hunt rabbits and go bird nesting, or even help working on the farm. We used to have a great time. If the weather was bad we would make up snares and mend the bolt nets for when we went ferreting. When the weather was better we would mend our tree hut. We always had something to do and something on the go.

Bob had started to whittle a bit of wood months ago with his penknife. He was making a dagger, it had taken him ages. But it was beginning to take shape and didn't look too bad. Any spare time he had he would be whittling away.

"It's a labour of love." Aunty May said. Dad said,

"You want to get something better to do with your time boy. A wooden knife is no good to anybody, it wouldn't cut butter."

Bob was undeterred and got some sandpaper from the sideboard drawer and started sanding it smooth.

"I'm going to take it to school on Monday and show it to my teacher and see what he thinks."

Anyway, Bob's Mum came and picked him up on Sunday night and took him back to Lockerbie for school the next morning and we said we would see him at the weekend. The next week seemed to fly past and when we were having our dinner on Saturday when Bob's Mum dropped him off for the weekend. He came running in the back kitchen waving his wooden dagger.

"How did you get on with the teacher, when you showed him your dagger?" Barnsey said.

"Oh great." Bob said. "He even wrote a message on it for me."

Everybody round the table having dinner looked impressed - even Dad.

"Well boy," he said to Bob, "let's have a look and see what he wrote."

Bob gave Dad the dagger and he pondered while reading the writing on the blade.

"Come on Dad. What did the teacher write?" I asked. Everybody else chirped in,

"Yeah, what does it say?"

Dad shuffled uneasily and read out.

Aunty May, Sandy the cat and Fred the ferret

George and me were playing around the back of the byre with the ferrets and dogs, to see if we could catch any rats underneath the cement bags and building material, at the end of the new byre and dairy.

It seemed like the builders had abandoned working on the buildings for the summer but I'm sure they hadn't, or Dad would have been right on their backs. The real reason for them not hurrying was that the electricity wasn't going to be connected for another couple of months. The bulk of the work had been done and all they had to do was things like put the roof on and fit the doors and windows.

The dogs jumped back and we ran to see if there were any rats but it was a false alarm. It was just Fred the Ferret poking his head out of the cement bags and into the daylight. The dogs never attacked the ferrets because they knew that, when the ferrets were there, usually it wasn't long before a rat appeared. But not this time.

I picked up Fred and put him under my jumper and George did the same with his ferret, when it appeared. We did that sometimes, especially if we hadn't got a hessian sack with us to put them in.

On the way back to where the ferret's cage was in the coal shed, we had to pass the back kitchen and we could hear Aunty May and Mum making the dinner and chatting away. We thought we would let one of the ferrets into the Kitchen to liven things up a bit. What we didn't know was that Sandy the cat was having a snooze in front of the Rayburn. Fred the Ferret had a sniff and went round the walls of the kitchen and then came to the Rayburn and a big ball of fluff - Sandy the cat. Fred stopped, sniffed and went into attack mode, feet well apart, his back slightly arched and tail straight out and quivering. A bit like a rattle snake but with no rattle.

He struck and it certainly woke Sandy the cat up. In what seemed like a millisecond, it turned on Fred and gave him such a boxing round the ears before running around all the walls of the kitchen. A bit like one of those motor bikes at the Fair in the Wall of Death. He tried to get out of the closed window, before flying out the back door and down the back yard.

Fred stood there, bewildered, in front of the Rayburn obviously thinking

"What the hell was that?"

George and me roared with laughter but not for long. The women folks, when they finally worked out what had happened went into their own attack mode. Aunty May with the kitchen brush shoeing Fred the Ferret out of the kitchen and Mum with the carpet beater, bending the bamboo on our backsides as we tried to escape running around the yard.

Finally the commotion died down and George and me caught Fred and I put him up my jumper and we walked round to the coal shed and put the both of them into their pen and gave them some milk and bread, plus a well-deserved rest.

After all the fuss in the kitchen we decided to steer clear of it for a while just in case. Standing at the door of the coal shed and wondering what to do till dinner time, we decided to go up to our tree hut and do some repairs that needed doing. Barnsey had told us to tie some of the boards we had up there with bits of binder twine and that would make it a lot safer, especially if we bound them and wrapped them real tight. So into the old byre we went. They always hung the binder twine on six inch nails to stop the cows getting it in their feed and choking.

We grabbed a bundle each and headed for our tree hut and started to do our tying, fixing and binding and, Barnsey was right, it was really easy to use and when you bound and tied it, it was really, really strong and when we finished it looked like a big crow's nest. But this was only the beginning. We had got plans for our tree hut.

It was dinner time so we headed to the back kitchen for our dinner and to face the music, hoping things might have calmed down. As we approached the back door, we could hear the men folks laughing and Aunty May trying to tell everybody about the ferrets. She said,

"It was horrible, just horrible, it stood there just looking at me with those horrible red eyes, I just got the brush and swept it clean out of the door and it smelt like high heaven."

Everyone just laughed at her and told her to get on with the dinner. On hearing that most of the folks in the back kitchen were on our side, we decided it was OK to pop our heads around the door, which we did, to a load of banter which didn't go down too well with Aunty May and Mum.

During dinner there were lots of stories all ending up with ferrets or cats which were getting up the noses Aunty May and Mum. In the end Mum turned round from the cooker sharply, which brought a sudden hush and looking at me she said,

"If you knew what happened to you when you were a baby, you wouldn't think running around the yard with a ferret up your jumper was very funny." Aunty May chirped in,

"Aye. That would knock the smiles off your faces. Bloody boys, frightening us like that." Mum went on,

"When you were a baby, just a couple of months old, you never stopped crying. You cried day and night. It was that bad in the end nobody took any notice of you. Anyway one day in June it was really hot and you were in your pram and we decided to put you in the shade of a tree at the bottom of the garden, while we had a cup of tea and a chat. Well you cried and cried and I said we should just leave you alone and you'll cry yourself to sleep. So we carried on drinking our tea and having a chat. The old sheepdog, without us knowing, had gone to investigate and she found a feral ferret had got into your pram and had got you by the throat and was worrying you. The dog jumped in the pram and grabbed the ferret and your Aunty May and me thought the dog was worrying you so we ran down the garden to get her off you. The pram fell over and everything fell out onto the grass. It was then that we realized the dog had got a wild ferret and was shaking the life out of it.

If it hadn't been for that old dog, that ferret would have killed you. It took several months for the teeth marks to disappear and that was the biggest ferret anybody had ever seen."

The scythe and binder

It was time to start harvesting. The Old Man told Sandy to get the Binder sorted out and ready for cutting the corn. He said that the rabbits had eaten loads of corn, especially around the headlands near the woods. He then sharpened up the scythe with the carborundum sharpening stone. He was going to scythe around the edge of the field and headlands before using the binder.

The Binders cutting blade was hung on the left hand side. If you didn't cut it with the scythe beforehand, the tractor and binders wheels would crush the corn down and it would just go to waste. Dad did not like waste.

He started scything. George and me were helping Barnsey rake up the newly cut corn and making it into sheaves, tying them up with a by tying a swathe of corn around them.

We put the sheaves at the side of the field so the tractor and binder could get past in the morning. Then we would make them into stooks as soon as the binder had been around a couple of times giving us more room to manoeuvre.

Sandy went to the farm and got the binder oiled and ready for reaping the corn in the morning. He also threaded a new ball of binder twine into the knotter after cleaning it.

Dad couldn't half scythe. He was nearly as fast as the tractor, the only difference being, the tractor didn't need a rest every now and then. He used to hide the fact he was knackered, by standing there sharpening the scythe, saying,

"You've got to have a sharp blade." Come teatime, Mum brought down to the field the enamel tea can full of tea and a load of freshly buttered scones. It was really welcome as everyone, including George and me, had been working quite hard, so we all sat down on the stubble and had a cup of tea, plus buttered scones and a chat. Dad was chatting to Barnsey and saying what it used to be like with Sandy agreeing with everything he said and nodding his head in approval. He reckoned in the old days everything was done by hand.

"But things are changing now," he said, "with electricity coming in the next couple of months and we won't be milking by hand any more. Most of the Sheep shearing was done with mechanical clippers this year. There won't be any hand shears at the clipping next year. You've got to move with the times, or get left behind. Down south they're cutting the corn with a thing called a combine harvester and bagging the grain in the field on the combine. That will be the next thing. You bet. The next thing you know, the threshing machine will be made redundant and Jimmy and Nughy will be looking for another job. You mark my words."

Then he finished his tea with one gulp and jumped up to go and start work and everyone else jumped up as well. If the Old Man jumped, everyone jumped, Mum said.

"Only, much higher," George said.

We worked really hard that afternoon and at about five o clock Barnsey went off to milk the cows, in the old byre. Sandy and George and me, carried on raking the corn into big heaps and making sheaves ready for stooking. When the Old Man had finished scything around the edge of the corn field, he mucked in with making sheaves and wrapping them and we soon had it done and finished, ready for the tractor and binder the next day.

At dinner that night we were all having a good laugh and larking about as usual and Sandy Carson said we should set a long net down at the bottom of the corn field and see if we could catch a few rabbits With the gap that was left where Dad had cut right round he field, the rabbits would be going into the long corn about now to feed and we could string the long net at the bottom of the field, between the wood and the corn. We were all for it. Dad and Sandy got the net out of the shed and went down to the bottom of the corn field to set it. We had to give them ten minutes or so and then we would beat the rabbits down to the end of the field and hopefully into the net.

The Old Man gave us a shout from the bottom of the field and we started off. We spread out. There was Barnsey on one side, George in the middle and me on the other side. The dogs were coursing the patch and we were shouting and making lots of noise to bolt the rabbits. It didn't take long. Just as quick as you could walk down the field there were quite a lot of them in the net. When we got there, we helped Dad and Sandy get them out of the net and wrung their necks and gutted them. We hung them up in the dairy and counted them. There were twenty two rabbits. Dad would take them to the market in Dumfries on Saturday.

The net was hung up on the shed wall again. All in all everybody had had a good evening. Bar the rabbits and it was still just half past eight.

After school the next day, we headed back to the farm as soon as Mrs. Leven had rang the bell, got changed, and headed down to the corn field. The Old Man was just finishing off the bindering and the corn left standing, was now a triangle in the middle of the field and getting smaller very quickly. There were no rabbits in the last bit so the dogs were had nothing to chase.

The binder twine had run out just before he finished but Dad just kept going because he couldn't be bothered to put a new roll of binder twine in the knotter just for half a dozen sheaves and the binder had thrown the sheaves out in bundles but not tied. So we bound them by hand.

After about an hour, all the stooking was done and the Old Man and Sandy started taking the binder and all the tools back to the barn, while George and me were playing hid and seek in amongst the stooks and sheaves.

The stooks would be left out in the field for a few days, or sometimes weeks, to ripen and dry, before being taken into the rick yard for the winter and the thrashing. What with a few bad days of weather and waiting for the stooks to dry properly, it was nearly a fortnight before we started clearing the stooks and building the new ricks in the rick yard. The gathering of the corn, commenced on a Friday with just a few of the men working on setting the bases of the ricks down, with the few sheaves they had brought in. A bit like a practice run for the next couple of days when we would try to get most of the harvest in and ricked in the yard.

It was the weekend and the Old Man had recruited as many folks as he could find, to try and get all the corn ricked up and in the yard, before the weather broke. He had got his mate Robert Cowen from Torthorwald, Jock Kirkpatrick from Shieldhill and Johnny the painter from Dumfries and several others.

Barnsey was building the ricks and to deliver the sheaves to him we had everything that you could working, even Old Meg the Clydesdale, was pulling the horse cart and the ricks were steadily going up. That's the hardest Barnsey had ever worked. It was relentless, when he thought he had beaten the rush and would get a little break, another corn cart would rattle into the yard and it was all go again.

Mum and Aunty May, were kept really busy in the back kitchen. There was no dinner as such, just a continuous stream of tea and sandwiches and scones, as the different carts come past the gate to the rick yard. The Old Man only gave Barnsey a break for twenty minutes, to have a cup of tea and get something to eat, so the whole rigmarole kept rolling on.

At the end of the weekend, most of the corn had been gathered, with just a few broken sheaves to pick up, probably half a trailer full. Barnsey and Sandy would get them the next day and tidy up all the loose ends. It was always a good time at harvest. It was even better to see the harvest gathered and safely stacked in the rick yard and good to see stillness in the air, with wisps of mist over the newly harvested fields and a great big harvest moon.

Another lesson John learnt

Chips the Terrier was a Pytchley Hunt Terrier, a bit like a Jack Russell but not so yappy. Brother John used to tease Chips, by pretend fighting with her. He used to clench his fists in and out and make a gurring sounds, forcing her back into the corner of the room. She would get really worked up, get out of the corner and run like a mad thing round the kitchen, out of the door and round the yard and come flying in the back door looking for more. She used to love it. It was all good fun and it kept her in trim for ratting and rabbiting.

One day at breakfast, John was still in his pajamas and had finished his breakfast first. He got up from the table and started teasing Chips, who had been lying quite happily in front of the Rayburn. She wasn't too happy at being forced out of her position in front of the warm cooker. Everyone at the table was moaning about the noise they were making and told him to pack it up as everyone was still finishing their breakfast. John said he was just playing with her and carried on but when the Old Man moaned he started to take notice. He took his eye off the dog and turned round to answer the Old Man

Chips, now in attack mode, grabbed John by the bollocks through his pajamas.

That really made his eyes water. Everyone at the table thought he had got his just desserts. Even though it was only breakfast time.

John and everyone else thought the worst. Mum was straight on the phone to Doctor Campbell from Lochmaben but thank goodness, it had only ripped his scrotum. The Doc was at the farm in no time and got him stitched up straight away. The Doctor told him he was very lucky.

I never saw him teasing Chips again. Nor have I ever seen him coming down in his pajamas for breakfast and I'm sure he wore two pairs of pants from then on. Once bitten twice shy!

The dynamite blasters

During the autumn gales, we had several trees along the Spring Burn felled by the strong winds. This would not normally have been a problem but the trees that had fallen were right on a bend in the burn. Its banks had been undermined over the past few years with previous flood waters. This had weakened the roots. There was a good chance that if we had a lot of rain in the winter they would dam the Burn and that would cause a lot of problems.

The Old Man got Barnsey and Sandy Carson to take the tractor and bogey trailer, loaded with saws, axes, log splitters and ropes. They also took a can of paraffin and a bale of old straw, to light fires to burn the small branches and any rotten wood and bark that was lying about.

George and me ran after the tractor as we went down the field to the Spring Burn. We had old Nell the Collie and Chips the Terrier with us too. The men started unloading the tools out of the back of the trailer while George and me were climbing all over the felled trees looking in all the cavities and nooks and crannies for old bird nests that were now much nearer the ground. There were no eggs or any other thing of much use to us. After all it was autumn.

The dogs were digging and sniffing about in the upturned roots which looked enormous. George said,

"They must call this time of the year the fall because it's when the trees get blown down to give us a load of logs for the winter." I agreed with him, while swinging from one of the branches over the burn, saying,

"You couldn't have the fall in Spring, because it would end up being Spring fall and Autumn up, it just wouldn't seem right would it" Before we could get further into the matter, Barnsey called us to give him a hand to start making a bonfire.

The Old Man and Sandy were sawing off the smaller branches into sizes that you could easily handle to make the base of the fire. Barnsey broke the old bale of straw open, removing about a third of it. We started building the fire, shaking up the straw so as to let the wind get through it, with Barnsey saying,

"That'll burn better all puffed up and loose like that." George and me started fetching the branches that had been sawn or chopped off which were by now, beginning to build up. Within half an hour we had a fair old bonfire ready to light.

The old Castrol can had about half a gallon of paraffin in it and Barnsey spread it liberally on the ready to light bonfire - especially on the straw. What we didn't realize, was that Barnsey had sneakily concealed the nearly empty five gallon can, with the lid firmly screwed back on, in the middle of the fire. He then lit it and immediately stood back.

At that moment, Mum arrived with a big can of tea and some buttered scones and the Old Man called for a tea break. As they walked up to where Mum was pouring out the tea, into colored, chipped, enameled tin mugs, from the chipped white enameled tea can, they gathered up the branches that had been cut and threw them on the fire. Barnsey, who with the thought of tea and scones had completely forgotten what he had done a few minutes earlier.

Mum had set the tea and scones out on the back of the bogey trailer parked at the top of the bank above the Burn, using it as a table. The bonfire was really going well now. You could feel the heat up at the tractor and trailer. Everyone was walking towards it to get their tea, all with their backs to the now roaring fire, which was about twenty yards from the trailer.

That's when it happened. With an eruption of fire and a sonic boom, a once square five gallon can, was now a bulging missile about fifty feet in the air, belching ignited vaporized paraffin, out of all of its newfound orifices. The next few seconds seemed to be in slow motion. Everything seemed to be surreal.

Because George and me were watching the men walk up from the Spring Burn to get their tea and were facing the fire when it exploded, we could see what was happening but the men couldn't, because it was behind them. They would normally have taken their time and assessed the situation but with this terrific noise going on behind them, assessment would have to wait and survival mode was put into action. Mum dropped the enamel tea can and started running up the field, shouting and screaming. The Old Man, Barnsey and Sandy Carson came past us at incredible speed. The Old Man was doing forward rolls. Barnsey fell over and was on all fours going like a scalded cat up the field. Sandy Carson, who had been rolling his fag at the time, came past us and it seemed like his feet, were moving faster than his body, but he was still rolling his fag.

It was at this time, out of the corner of my eye, a bit of a blur attracted my attention. It was the two dogs. They were going like the clappers. The collie was in front, very closely followed by the terrier. At first I thought they were chasing a rabbit, or hare but they were heading straight for the wood at the back of the Steadings farm and making for the safety of home.

In what seemed like the blink of an eye, real time resumed, with an eerie silence but only for a moment. The Old Man started first.

"Who the bloody hell done that" he shrieked. Looking at me and George and starting to purposely walk towards us to give us a good spanking. Barnsey, realizing what had happened, shouted out to the Old Man,

"No Tom, no Tom. It wasn't them, it wasn't them. It was me. I done it just for the laugh, and got distracted and completely forgot about it when Peg came down with the tea'.

"You silly bugger." Dad said, "It's a wonder that nobody's had a heart attack. Don't piss about like that again or I'll give you a bloody good kick up the arse." By this time, everyone was back at the trailer and getting over the trauma of the last few moments. Mum, luckily enough, had poured the tea before the fracas had occurred and when she dropped the can, it was nearly empty, so everybody had a mug of tea, although some ash had fallen in some of them. A bit of banter went on for a minute or two and Barnsey took the brunt of all the slagging off.

Then the Old Man and Sandy went back to sawing off branches. They were attempting the larger ones now, using a big band saw with one man on each end, to put more power into the job. Mum was clearing up the mugs and pots and putting them in the basket for the walk home to make the dinner and look for the dogs. George and me were told, to carry on helping Barnsey making up the fire. No bale of straw or paraffin this time. George went down the bank of the Burn to get the old and very battered Paraffin can back. It was still a very hot can, so he picked it up by sticking a couple of big twigs in the holes and walking up to the fire to shown us. Barnsey said.

"It must have been some force to do that." We started then to do our main job of building up the fire and clearing the small braches that the Old Man and Sandy were sawing. They were now getting to the thicker branches and we had to pull them up to the top of the bank with the tractor and ropes, ready to load onto the trailer to take them back to the yard. There they would we cut up with the circular saw for logs for the fires in the winter.

The work continued for two or three days. The branches that could be removed or burnt had come to an end and all that was left was three gigantic tree trunks and even with a big band saw it was a losing battle. That's where Ronnie Shuttleworth comes into the story. He reminded Dad that Kingan's saw mill in New Abbey had a couple of blasters working for him and if he rang Jimmy up he would send them over and they'd got all the tools and gear to do the job. It was all arranged for the next weekend. All they had to do was cut the tree trunks into three sections, ready for blasting and splitting the trunks into smaller pieces, so they could be pulled back to the yard with the crawler.

George and me could hardly wait for Saturday to come round. We had never seen anything blown up before. On that Saturday morning, at half past seven, the two blasters arrived ready to go. Mums' offer of cups of tea and fried bacon and egg sandwiches were eagerly accepted and then it was down the field to start work. Barnsey was told to stick to the milking and if he has got any spare time, to start mucking out a couple loose boxes and in general keep out of the way. They let us go down to watch them get the tree trunks ready for blasting but we were told that when they say we had to go, it meant we definitely had to go and no messing. They had big hand wood drills and they picked certain parts of the trunk and drilled quite deep, to insert the dynamite. We watched for a while and then we were told to scarper. So we went back to the farm and into the back kitchen to have some dinner and told Mum and Aunty May that we were going to watch from the road on the way to Fernieclough and it was far enough away and quiet safe. The men had said they were going to do the blasting about two o'clock, or thereabouts, so you know when to expect the bang.

"We'll give you a hoot on the Claxton, just before we blast." They had said. Straight after dinner George and me headed off down to the bridge over the burn where we were going to meet the Telfer Boy's and Graham Kirkpatrick. We were a little bit early, so we started climbing trees to pass the time and found out that we had a great view the higher we climbed. We must have looked like a pack of monkeys and for a while we forgot about the blasters. Then we heard the Claxton. So we all looked down to where the tree trunks were and hung on. Just then we saw old Nell, the Old Man and Sandy walking down the field to watch the blasting. Then one of the blasters bent down over this little square box and pushed the lever down. We were all watching the man with the small box and not where the tree trunks were. It was funny sort of noise. It wasn't a bang but more like a crack, followed by a boom, that sort of echoed around the fields and hills. We all sort recoiled with the shock, holding on to braches to keep our balance. That's where George got it wrong. The branch he

59

was holding onto was dead and well rotten. But the branch didn't hold onto the tree. After a quick backwards summersault, he landed on the banks of the burn, still clutching the branch.

The blasters had done all the three tree trunks at the same time. The trunks were well and truly split into manageable chunks that could be easily towed back to the farm yard by the David Brown crawler. We got George up the bank of the burn, by pulling him up over the edge with the old branch he was still clutching and we all walked down to the site where they had done the blasting. It stank of gunpowder and things were still smoking from the blast. Over the next few days, the logging area was cleared and eventually life got back to more or less normal but we did have a few problems with the dogs. The Old Man was rounding up the ewes to put to the rams in November but when they were near where the trees had been cleared, Old Nell wouldn't bring the sheep back if they were down the bottom of the field. She would go half way and then not move for anything. She couldn't get Barnsey's paraffin bomb out of her mind and I don't think I ever saw her go near the bottom of the field again, nor did Chips unless you carried him. But the Old Man always said,

"Where there's a will there's a way." His way was for George and me to do it. After a few days, we were nearly as good as Old Nell at rounding up the sheep.

Picking spuds

Around the middle of October we used to pick the potatoes. There were probably a couple of acres. This always coincided with the school half term and everyone who was fit, or nearly fit, was obliged to go to the local farms and help with the tattie picking. Come the Monday morning, the Old Man took the wee grey Fergie and the bogie trailer and went down to the school and picked up his allotted tattie houkers. A right motley crew but it was only for a few days. There were four kids and two Mums, The mothers just wanted to earn a few extra bob and they always got a carrier bag of spuds to take home with them. There was also me and George.

When they arrived at the tattie field, Barnsey took the pickers and stepped out about ten or twelve yards for each. That was their allotted pitch which was marked with a stone. The youngsters pitch was a bit shorter. After all some of us were only nine or ten. The way it worked was like this.

The Old Man drove the tattie digger, which was pulled by the wee grey Fergie. Sandy Carson was in charge of the tattie pit which was down at the bottom of the field near the gate, so that when they dug the spuds out in the winter, they didn't have to go too far from the road and get bogged down in all the mud. The pits were then covered with old straw and earth - a bit like thatching a roof. This was to keep out the rain and bad weather, especially the frost. It could get pretty cold up here in the winter. Old Meg the Clydesdale shire was hitched up to the two wheeled cart and she was used to walk up and down the drills and Barnsey picked up and emptied the baskets of spuds that had been picked by the women and kids into the cart and took them down to Sandy for the pit.

Barnsey made sure George and me were kept well apart. I was at one end of the pickers and George was at the other. The reason was so the Old Man who was driving the digger, could check we were working hard. The whole thing was orchestrated by the Old Man. When he started digging woe betide anyone who upset the system.

There was about ten of us picking and we all had to stand back while the tractor and digger came past. It had a big coulter with a spinner to break up the soil and expose the spuds and as soon as he came past your position in the row, you had to start picking like mad to fill the baskets. After a while picking, your back would start to ache but every time you thought you might get a rest, the old bugger came chugging past with the digger spewing loads of spuds at your feet. The only rest we got was when Mum came down at half past twelve and brought a couple of enamel cans full of tea and a bag of buttered scones and some shortbread - all homemade of course. Half an hour was all we had and then it was back to work.

Finally it was the last drill for the day. Well not really a day, because the Old Man had to take the women and kids back to the school for half past three to keep to school hours. Anyway, down the drill he chugged for the last time and when he got to the end of the drill, he unhitched the digger and hitched the bogie trailer to the tractor, ready for the school run. Barnsey was picking up the wire baskets full of spuds and emptying into the cart that old Meg was pulling. Nearly the end of a perfect day but not quite. George decided to liven things up a bit.

Old Meg was just passing with Barnsey tipping the baskets into the cart, when George blew the biggest raspberry ever and old Meg, who always bolted when you made a farting sound, was off, like a scalded cat, heading for the gate and then her stable. There were shouts of whoa, whoa, from Barnsey but to no avail, as we all stood there watching her charge down the field towards the gate with spuds bouncing over the side and back of the cart. Luckily Sandy was down at the pit next to the gate and came to the rescue by standing in front of the gate and catching her and calming her down.

Barnsey was still standing there holding his basket, looking bewildered but not for long. He cast an eye on George and George made a run for it but Barnsey was like a greyhound and ran him down in seconds, then gave him a good hiding he would never forget, at least for a week anyway until the next time.

Then all the pickers lined up next to the bogie trailer to get paid and then get a lift back to the school at Shieldhill. I'll never forget the Old Man counting out the money on the back of the bogie trailer. I'm sure he begrudged every penny and he made sure they got lots of pennies, half pennies, or even farthings to make it look like they had more than they actually had, which wasn't much anyway. The women got five bob and the kids got half a crown and George and me got thrupence, a good lecture and told to stop farting about. We were then told to get a basket each and pick up all the spuds that had fallen out of the cart when George had spooked old Meg. He wanted it done before he got back from dropping the pickers back to the school. He then looked at one of the women who was trying to get her free bag of spuds on the back of the bogey and said she had too many in the bag and made her empty some of them out. Nobody got a free ride out of the 'Old Man'.

After a few more days, the tattie hauking was over for another year. George and me were very glad to see an end of it. We hated it.

The head butter

Dad had got a couple of new rams or tups as we called them. That made seven tups altogether. He said that you have to keep introducing new blood into the flock and improve the strain all the time and those two rams were from good stock. When he had bought them at the Castle Douglass ram sale, he had also got some good luck money from the old farmer who sold them to him. The old farmer had said,

"Tom these two tups have that much spunk in them, you'll probably be able to rest the others and save on your raddle grease." There was no doubt about it. Dad was quite chuffed with his new purchases. This was mid-October and he wouldn't put the tups to the ewes, afore the second week in November. All the tups were kept in the paddock behind the byre until then and fed for the next few weeks to get there stamina up. There was no doubt about it. They had first class treatment for the task ahead. The Old Man fed them and made sure their feet were trimmed and their tails dagged, until in the end they were in tip top, Tup condition, ready for the ewes. He didn't want them to get amongst the ewes too early, because he wanted the ewes to lamb at the end of March after the bad weather. Barnsey the herdsman said.

"If you looked after us as good as you looked after those bloody tups, you might get a bit more work out of us." The Old Man said,

"The fastest I've ever seen you move Barnsey is when you hear the old tin can being banged for dinner. You do your job and I'll do mine, OK." With just another week to go, the routine was the same. Every morning and every night, the Old Man went down to the paddock, to make sure they got their hay and he would feed them some cake. Each one individually got their fair share. I don't think Dad had any favourites but the two new tups seemed to be doing well. One day he was feeding them as usual and shaking out the cake into little heaps in front of each one in turn and when he came to the last one, he bent down to shake out the last stuff from the bottom of the bag. One of the tups thought he was throwing down the gauntlet for a head butting competition. They never refuse a challenge as Dad was about to find out. He was just starting to stand up, when it hit him straight in the face. At that moment he found out what the phrase 'being rammed' meant.

Luckily he didn't have his head right down and it didn't contact skull to skull, or it might have killed him. Hitting him in the face didn't do too much damage. Just a broken nose, a couple of teeth knocked out and a black and blue face. Plus his pride. But what annoyed him most was, when he finally got up from the ground, wanting to give the tup that butted him a good hiding with his knobbly stick, he couldn't, because he didn't know which one had rammed him.

He had to go to a dance that weekend and looked a right mess, black and blue, two teeth missing. We stood in the back kitchen to see him and Mum off. Barnsey quipped,

"You should have raddled them tups early. If you'd dabbed a bit of raddle on their foreheads, you would have known which one had butted you"

Sandy Carson said,

"If you were the other way round Tom you might have been the first one lambing next March." For the next few days, until we put them to the ewes, Barnsey fed the Tups, being careful not to bend down, either way.

The Standard Ford crash

In bad weather, just before it got really cold and all the cattle were brought down to the shelter of the farm buildings for the winter, we would supplement the now meager grass resources with old hay from last year's crop and some chopped up turnips. Just for a couple of weeks or so before the beasts came down. This was done with the old Standard Ford and the bogey trailer. The Old Man used to drive the tractor and Barnsey used to stand on the bogey and fork out the fodder to the beasts. They used to always run beside the trailer mooing until Barnsey started throwing the hay and turnips over the side.

On Monday morning, George and me went to school and started a new week, with the usual gusto. All went well but, half way through the afternoon, Davey Marshal from one of the neighboring farms came to the school and told Mrs. Leven to keep me and George at the school after the classes finished. There had been an accident and they didn't want us to see it or get in the way. So at the school we had to stay.

Meanwhile on the farm there was a major rescue operation going on. What had happened was that The Old Man and Barnsey had been feeding the cattle on the highest field on the hill and everything was going alright until they started to head for home. The old Standard Ford was old and it wasn't really made for working on steep hills. We thought it must have been the first tractor invented after the steam engine. It had a big springy metal seat on the back of on which we used to put a hessian bag with some hay or straw in as a cushion. The controls were pretty basic, a hand throttle, a metal steering wheel about the size of a dustbin lid and a clutch and brakes on the same pedal. That was the cause of the problem. You pushed the peddle half way down and the clutch took the power off the engine but then it free wheeled till you pushed the peddle further down and the brakes come on. In theory anyway. The problem was that you were supposed to balance the brakes up, so they both came on at the same time and no one could remember the last time they had been adjusted. Not this side of the WW II anyway.

So when the Old Man and Barnsey had finished feeding the cattle and were on their way home, instead of going back home the safe way, down the old track that had been there since Roman times, he decided to take a short cut straight down the hill to save time. It certainly got to the bottom of the field a lot quicker. But not the way intended. The Old Man and Barnsey who had old Nell on the trailer with him, gradually picked up speed and he decided to put it down a gear for the really steep part. Big mistake. He put it out of third gear to move it down to second gear but to no avail. Barnsey said he thought that the Old Man was doing an Irish jig on the back of the tractor trying to double de-clutch but into gear it wouldn't go. The Old Man shouted for Barnsey to jump for it. Barnsey didn't need telling twice. He was gone followed immediately by old Nell. Just in time, because with all the bumping about the pin in the drawbar jumped out and the bogie parted company with the tractor. The drawbar of the bogie dug into the ground and it somersaulted down the hill behind the old Standard Ford which by this time was completely out of control. The Old Man was desperately trying to regain some control but to no avail. He eventually decided to abandon the tractor but he made a bad decision. He tried to jump uphill to prevent the tractor rolling over him. But the tractor slewed round out of control, the large mudguard caught him as it rolled and took him back and crushed him on the first of its many rolls. They later said, that if he had jumped the other way, he would have rolled clear. But that was not to be.

Because the accident happened on the high hill field, loads of the neighbors had witnessed it happen and a rescue mission was put in action. That's why George and me were kept at school. The Old Man had broken ribs and a broken pelvis and other minor injuries. He spent six weeks in the Infirmary at Dumfries and just as long recuperating when he came home. Barnsey had just a few bruises but said later that it had put the shits right up him when it happened and he had to do lots more work with the Old Man in the Hospital.

Old Nell was unhurt as far as anyone could see and Barnsey said that, after the accident, she went up to where the Old Man was lying and licked his face. Apparently the old tractor rolled and bounced over five times, before coming to a halt.

A bad decision day for the Old Man. It was the talk of the area for weeks.

The parachute

George and me were kicking about the back kitchen wondering what to do. Mum and Aunty May told us to go and give Barnsey the herdsman a hand milking the coos and to get out from under their feet so they could get on preparing the dinner.

We went down the back yard and into the byre. Barnsey was halfway through the milking and said he didn't want a hand and to go and do something else and get out from under his feet because these new heifers were a bit twitchy. If he didn't watch out he could get a good kicking, trying to get the milking units on. So we just stood in the paddock next to the sheep dip bunging bits of cattle feed into the water, watching green slimy bubbles come slowly to the surface. Then we decided to go to the Telfer's at Ferniclough to play with Robert and Austin Telfer because they had told us at school that while rummaging through their uncle Bob's out house, they had found some of his old Army gear and amongst it was a white desert helmet, a gas mask and a big greenish parachute.

When we got there, they had just finished having their tea and their Mum wanted them out of the house because she was sewing up Mr. Telfer's dungarees that got ripped when the old bull gave chase. He just made it over the gate in time but got caught on a nail and ripped the arse out of them. So she didn't want to be bothered with folks around.

We headed for the barn where Robert and Austin had hidden their Uncle Bobs Army gear under some bales of hay and we all had a go at wearing the white desert helmet and gas mask, George ended up marching up and down the barn with the hat and gas mask on at the same time doing Nazi salutes and shouting in a muffled voice 'Heil Hitler,' to everyone's amusement. We then turned our attention to the parachute, spreading it out in the barn and trying to figure out how to use it.

In the end we decided on the barn roof, it had to be the highest and best launching pad. At one end of the barn there was a big heap of loose coal and slag. It was only about twenty foot from the top of the roof to the heap of slag and if the parachute didn't open, it would be a soft landing for the jumper. We climbed up over a couple of lower roofs to gain access to the main barn roof, dragging the parachute behind us. When we looked down it looked a lot higher but at least it would be a softish landing. It was decided George should go first because he was the lightest. He didn't want to but we insisted it had to be him. He finally agreed so we hitched him into the parachute harness and got him on the edge ready for the jump. We spread the parachute out behind George and Bob went back down to help at the landing site. George was just waiting for the green light. If he survived, we told him, he would be hero.

Everything was in position for takeoff and landing. Bob was standing by at the slag heap, Austin was in charge of the takeoff, holding the parachute open to catch the wind and so on. I was in charge of being in charge, I suppose. George was the test pilot or was it the dummy. Yes it was well organized. We had spent at least ten minutes working things out to the finest detail. We knew precisely nothing about what was going to happen to George. Neither did George but he liked surprises.

I lifted my hand shouting to everyone to get ready for the jump or, should I say, leap of faith, but in the end it was more like a hop. I dropped my hand and George just hopped off the end of the barn and then dropped straight into the slag heap. He sort of hopped and dropped and wasn't too happy with his first test flight. He landed feet first in the slag heap and sank up to his knees in the slag and coal and it filled his wellie boots full of dross. He couldn't pull his feet out of the slag or the wellies but luckily Bob was on hand to help him out but they were both covered in dross and coal dust.

Austin was still standing in the launch position, holding the end of the parachute, shaking it like a table cloth. I don't think he had realized George had hopped it. We eventually began to analyse what had gone wrong with our meticulous planning. The one thing we realized straight away was the need for more height because with the barn being twenty foot high and the slag heap being five foot high and the parachute being at least thirty foot when stretched out, we had got our sums wrong. What we needed was a steep hill or something a lot higher than the barn.

We got George and Bob cleaned up in the byre, packed the parachute into a bag, with the helmet and gas mask and started thinking and planning, how to get airborne. There had to be a way.

When we got back home from the Telfer's Barnsey had finished the milking and was just brushing the byre out and swilling it down with buckets of water, ready for milking in the morning. We told him what had happened with the parachute. He listened and after having a good laugh, we all sat down on some bales of straw and analyzed everything all over again, to see what had gone wrong. Barnsey was nearly twice our age and he knew everything, or so we thought. He told us that his uncle Angus was in the Para's during the war and that when they started their training, they jumped off a big tower before they jumped out of a plane. It was at least a hundred foot high and specially built for the job. We knew we couldn't build anything that big. The only thing I could think of was the steep hill at the back of the old Roman fort. It's so steep you can't walk on it. If it was any steeper it would be a cliff and it had to be at least a hundred feet or more.

We all agreed that was a good idea and we would try it out one day soon. Barnsey then added that his Uncle Angus said they used to do training towed behind a jeep or army lorry. Just to get used to take off and landing. We could do that with the wee grey Fergie George piped in. It must do at least ten miles an hour, maybe more. Aye Barnsey said,

"You might just manage it with that but I think the hill at the back of the old Roman fort would be the best one to try first. The Old Man isn't going to think too much of it if he catches you roaring around the field on the tractor. Wait until there's a decent day with not too much wind, then give it a go.

Just then we heard Mum banging the old tin bucket at the back kitchen door with the poker calling us in for supper. She didn't have to bang it too long when it concerned food. Aunty May was at the table buttering up some freshly cooked scones singing her little la de da songs, Mum was filling up the teapot with boiling water. Dad and Grandpa were already sitting down in their chairs, eating scones after spreading loads of bramble jam on them. There's no doubt about it. Mum and Aunty May knew how to put a spread on. It was seldom that anyone was late for supper or any other meal come to think of it.

Snaring rabbits with Grandpa

Grandpa John was saying he had set a load of snares up the back of the hill and along the wire fence at the Telfer's bogey wood. He said the rabbits were taking over up there, there's that many of them. They're eating the crops round the edges of all the fields and swarming all over the hill.

"They're breeding like rabbits," he retorted. Everyone was roaring with laughter, except Grandpa, He didn't like being the butt of the joke but finally started laughing too. When we all calmed down Grandpa asked George and me if we wanted to go first thing in the morning to check the snares for rabbits so Dad could take them to the market on Saturday morning. He's getting two bob a pair for them now, so it's well worth the time to get a few bob extra. We were all up for it.

"Yeah Grandpa, wake us up in the morning and we'll come with you and give you a hand."

"Come on boys." Aunty May said, "If you're going in the morning you had better get off to your bed. Early to bed. Early to rise. Get up the golden stairs and get to sleep and it'll be morning in no time." Sure enough it seemed like the blink of an eye and Grandpa was standing at the bedroom door telling us to hurry up and get up and we'll have breakfast when we get back down from the hill. He then strode out of the back kitchen door, saying,

"Come on boy's. Its half past six and we want to be back by half eight." He then got on the wee grey Fergie with the bucket on the back and told us to hang on and off we went. We had to go through the paddock to get onto the track that runs up to the old Roman fort. George and me took it in turns to open and shut the gates. We sat on some hessian sacks in the bucket on the back of the tractor with our legs dangling over the back, chatting away about the parachute and how we could have a look at the steep hill when we got to the Fort.

The sun was just rising over the back of the hill. It was the earliest we had been up in ages and there were wisps of mist in the hollows. The gorse bushes and long grass had thousands of spider's webs caressing the undulating hillsides, glistening in the now quickly rising sun.

We went over the brow of the hill and the old Fort came into sight. He had set the snares pegged into the ground and the loop of the snare was held up by a twig over the run and the rabbit would hop along the run and sometimes stick its head in it. Sometimes it would flatten it and just run on past. We reached a big patch of bracken and gorse bushes where Grandpa had set the first lot of snares.

We drew up beside one of the snared rabbits and switched the tractor off. Grandpa, clutching his big knobbly stick, jumped off the tractor and whacked it behind the ears. He then got his backy knife out and paunched it there and then, throwing the guts away from the run. He threw the rabbit into the bucket on the back of the tractor before resetting the snare. There were rabbits scooting everywhere, sometimes stopping with their ears cocked, looking towards us through the early morning mist before heading for their burrows, or the bracken and gorse bushes.

There were some rabbits that didn't run and hide, they were the ones that had been snared and were just sitting there waiting to meet their fate. Grandpa's knobbly stick. There was no reprieve, not at two bob a pair. After awhile, we had done all the snares and George and me were gutting the rabbits, while Grandpa was resetting the snares. We were also having a good look at the steep hill at the back of the old fort. It looked ideal for the parachute.

We finished the paunching about the same time Grandpa finished resetting the snares. We then headed off for the Telfers bogey wood. On arriving there the sun was getting well up in the sky but the trees were casting a shadow all along the boundary fence. It was still damp along the fence in the shade. Grandpa had set the snares along the wood by tying them onto one of the wires of the five wired boundary fence. There were loads of runs. Some of them were concealed with tufts of grass but they were easy to find and Grandpa didn't miss many.

When we had a look along the fence, it looked like he had been quite successful. Some of the rabbits had clapped down and stayed dead still, hoping not to be seen. A couple had struggled and jumped through the wires of the fence and hung themselves. As we went further on along the fence we heard a rabbit screeching as though in pain and George and me ran on to see what all the noise was about and came upon a rabbit that was snared. A stoat had it by the throat and wouldn't let go. It had got the taste of blood and wasn't scared of George or me but thought better of it when Grandpa appeared out of the mist with his big knobbly stick, banging the ground with it shouting

"That's my Rabbit, go and catch your own rabbit, you little bugger." It shot off into the edge of the wood and stood there in a sort of defiant stance, waiting just in case it might get another chance but Grandpa and the knobbly stick won the day .George and me both felt sorry for that rabbit, snared with a stoat hanging on its throat, then getting whacked on the back of the head with a big knobbly stick. We preferred chasing them with the dogs and giving them half a chance and most of them would get away. But the older folks had just been through the War and food was food and we still had got ration books. After that George and me never used snares. We stuck to chasing.

When we finished gutting the rabbits and setting the snares, we bagged up the rabbits and headed down the hill and eventually pulled up next to the old dairy. Grandpa shouted to Mum and Aunty May who were in the back kitchen, to get the eggs and bacon on while we unloaded the rabbits and hung them up in the dairy. We had stuck the knife through the back legs just above the tendons when we gutted them so that we could knit their legs together and hang them on the wooden poles that were strung across the dairy. It took about a quarter of an hour to hang them up and, when we counted them, we had got thirty seven. Grandpa looked quite happy with our early morning's work. We ended up with a big fried breakfast and I had a double yolked egg and it was still just gone nine.

Most importantly, George and me had got a good look at the steep hill at the back of the old fort and now we could organize another parachute jump.

Two old fools and their money are soon parted

Come Saturday morning the Old Man had over a hundred rabbits to take to the market in Dumfries. When they loaded the old Austin pickup truck with the rabbits, they just left them on the wooden poles. They fitted straight in the back under the canvas cover and that was about as much as you could get in the old Austin. Grandpa decided to go to Dumfries with the Old Man and we all cheerily waved them off from the back yard. It was all smiles and a happy start to a lovely day, a day with lots of promise, of things to come. Mum and Aunty May went back to work, feeding the hens, churning and making butter and preparing the dinner for tonight. George and me went to play in the tree hut and do a few repairs, to the roof.

The time just seems to fly past, when you're enjoying yourselves and in what seemed to be next to no time, we heard a commotion in the back yard and ran round from the wood to see what was happening. It was the Old Man and Grandpa. They were back and had been enjoying themselves too. They had been drinking. Grandpa couldn't get out of the van and the Old Man was staggering around the yard. Mum and Aunty May were at the back kitchen door and they weren't too happy at the sight before them. The van was here. The rabbits were gone. Dad and Grandpa were here, at least in body, but I think their souls were still in the Market Tavern in Dumfries. The Old Man wandered off down the yard, to get out of the earshot of Mum and Aunty May and the ensuing storm.

Mum reckoned they hadn't got a brain between them and that there was more sense in an old brush head. Aunty May was saying,

"That's right Peg. You get the two of them together and they're just like two daft kids. You give them too much credit saying a brush head. They must have wasted at least ten bob, on their lust for alcohol. It's just terrible, just terrible."

George and me decided to go and see if Dad was alright. As we walked past the van, Grandpa seemed to have succumbed to gravity and was slumped in the passenger seat with his pipe in one hand and his balls in the other. We continued down to the bottom of the yard to see where the

Old Man had got to and there he was, hanging onto a fence with hands, retching and spewing into the sheep dip. We decided to leave him alone and headed for our tree hut and some peace and quiet. Upon walking back past the Van, Grandpa was still there but had changed hands and had got a little smile on his face. Mum and Aunty May were still going at it hammer and tongs and as we walked past the back kitchen, it was,

"A fool and his money are soon parted. The brains of a brush head," Mum said.

"An old one." said Aunty May.

It was several days before things finally calmed down and got back to normal

Another parachute jump

We went to school on Monday and started planning the next parachute jump. Schoolwork was decidedly second. We finally decided to give the parachute the green light for the coming Saturday, when the Old Man and Grandpa would be at the market in Dumfries.

Saturday soon come round and, as soon as Grandpa and the Old Man went off to the market, the Para group began to appear from where they had been waiting, out of sight, in the wood and hedges. Robert and Austin had brought the parachute, the gas mask and the white African helmet with them. There were six of us altogether. Tim had come on his bike from Lochmaben and Graham from Shieldhill, plus George and me.

Barnsey was at the paddock gate, when we started our trek up to the Old Fort. He said he had to check the Galloway hill cattle later on and they were up near the old Fort and he would have a look in on us, if he had the time. We headed up the track chatting away and throwing stones at thistles and fence posts, or any other thing we could find to use as a target. There was no sense of urgency as we ambled along. We had a couple of diversions to chase rabbits but they were far too quick for us and soon disappeared down their burrows to safety. We hadn't brought the dogs with us because we didn't want to have them get tangled up with the parachute or get in the way. I don't think they would have caught the rabbits anyway.

We arrived at the bottom of the Old Fort and walked around the bottom and looked at the steepest bits and decided to go up to the top for a better look. We couldn't climb the steep parts but either side of it the incline reduced to a gentle slope, so we could maybe have a few practice runs.

When we got to the top, we went over to the steep part to have a look. George had a look and said,

"No way am I going down there, with or without a parachute." We all looked down and came to the same conclusion as George but then Bob said,

"Why don't we practice on a not so steep part? It won't be quite so dangerous. George said,

"That would be a good idea Bob, you can go first." After a bit of banter we got Bob into the harness and we all walked to the not so steep part. We spread the parachute out behind Bob and he took up the strain on its lines. Then two of us spread the parachute to catch the wind and Bob started running - well fast walking. We were just about to get some air in the canopy when the slope went from downhill to uphill and the canopy collapsed with Bob collapsing beside it saying it was, far too much like hard work and someone else should have a go, until he got his breath back.

In the end we all had a go except George, who was feeling a bit left out by this time. We had been edging towards the steeper parts of the hill but we hadn't had a good takeoff yet although Tim got a bit of wind in the canopy and managed a hop skip and plop. All this time George had been feeling a bit left out of it and because he was the one who was usually at the centre of attention he wanted to have the next go.

We made our way to the top of the ridge and got George into the harness. He insisted on going down the steep part and also insisted on wearing the white helmet and the gas mask but after a minute he threw it on the floor, saying he couldn't stand the smell of the old rubber and we should get on with it. So we all took up our positions, Bob and me holding the parachute out to try and catch the wind and the rest of them down at the bottom of the hill ready to catch George who was by this time raring to go. He looked the part with his big white African helmet on. He took up the strain and Bob and me held the parachute up and he started running as we tried to catch the wind and then let him go.

He was doing a sort of falling sort of run and jump. We were all shouting and cheering but it was a nearly but not quite and George stood at the bottom of the hill with the parachute hanging half inflated, hanging limply from his back. We were just about to un-harness him, when a sudden gust of wind filled the parachute and he was gone. He was running up the hill faster than he ran down it and when he got to the top of the hill, the wind seemed to drop and George started running back down the hill. When he was nearly at the bottom, another gust of wind grabbed the parachute and George was on his way back up the hill again. This repeated itself several times. He was completely out of control and going up and down the hillside. Just like a yoyo.

We tried several times to catch him but every time we were about to grab him, the wind snatched him from us. It seemed strongest at the bottom of the gulley and it knew exactly when to whip him away and out of our grasp. In what proved to be his last run up the steep face, his white African helmet came off and rolled down the hill, bouncing and rolling all over the place. We all ran over to get the helmet which was slowly spinning to a stop. The inner lining of the helmet was an olive green color and the strap was a light brown and everybody wanted to try it on and for a moment or two, we completely forgot about George. When we looked to see where he was, he was nowhere in sight and nowhere to be found. There was a short pause of realization, then blind panic as everyone climbed to the top of the hill to see what had happened to George.

Unbeknown to us, when we were all busy catching the helmet and trying it on, Barnsey, who had been checking the hill cattle, was walking over the brow of the hill when George had popped up. Barnsey had grabbed him and held him till he got everything under control and wrapped up the parachute and got George out of the harness - all out of sight of us. They then decided to run away and hide from us taking the parachute with them. By the time we got ourselves up the top of the hill, they were half way home and well out of sight.

The wind was getting up a bit now and there was no George in sight and our merry group was at a complete loss. George has just disappeared, vanished, gone. We started scanning the skies looking to see if he was still airborne and maybe flying towards the Solway Firth, or gliding over the hills and glens towards Queensbury and the Lead Hills at Moffat. But he was nowhere in sight'

"He won't be flying against the wind." Tim said. "Wherever he's gone, there's only one way and that's downwind. He was the lightest one of all of us".

"You're right." Graham said. "If we throw some grass in the air, it'll show us which way the wind is blowing."

We all came to the same conclusion. The wind was blowing straight towards the Telfers boggy wood. We spread out and headed down towards the wood, searching the patches of ferns and gorse and looking for any remnants of the parachute, or George, come to think of it. All the time, shouting 'George, George.'

Grahame said,

"We should have brought the dogs with us," they would have sniffed him out, "the little bugger."

After finding nothing on the way down to the wood, we entered the entanglement of trees, some dead some alive, and spread out about fifty yards apart and started combing the area, shouting 'George' but maybe a bit louder. After about an hour we had searched the wood and everyone was glad, because no one liked being alone in the boggy wood too long. We gathered around to try and work out what to do next. We decided to go back home and get help. Started off down the hill, hoping we might find George on the way.

On arriving in the backyard, we gingerly walked up towards the back kitchen door, to be met by Barnsey. The Old Man and Grandpa, who had arrived back from the Market, half an hour earlier, were there too. The Old Man said,

"I've got a message for George from his Mum. She was at the market in Dumfries and wanted me to pass it on to him. Where's George boys?" Barnsey said,

"He was with you when you went up the hill this morning."
I muttered to everyone standing there,

"We think we've lost him. We think he's blown away in the parachute, because we've searched everywhere and can't find him. All we've got left, is the gas mask and the big white desert helmet, but no George."

We thought they would go mad at George being missing but they didn't seem to bother too much and were just chatting away with each other and saying things like,

"Nobody will miss him," and, "he was a bloody pest anyway." Grandpa said, "His Mum might miss him for a while but she would soon get over it. Time is a great healer. It was then that Austin spotted a green heap in the corner, next to the back door. It was the parachute.

"Look. That's the parachute. That's the parachute." He shouted. "If that's the parachute, then George must be here somewhere as well." We all started looking for George and it didn't take long to track him down. There he was in the back kitchen, cowering behind Grandpa's chair, underneath the wireless, sitting there with a silly grin on his face.

The men then told us that they were standing in the yard and someone looked up towards the hill and thought they had spotted a big bird flying down the side of the hill and as it got nearer we realized it was George and he was flying, just like a bird and he landed on the Barn roof.

"Yes, he flew down the side of the hill. Swooped over the paddock and landed on the barn roof, just like a big bird." Grandpa said, with everybody, including George, nodding their heads and murmuring in agreement at this miraculous achievement of aviation. We felt a bit left out and peeved at having missed out on George's amazing endeavors.

After giving us a lecture on safety and saying that we should have had George tethered, preferably by the neck. They said that if George hadn't been such a good and natural flier, due to him reading loads of Biggles books and if the wind had been blowing in a different direction it, could have been a very different story.

"All's well that ends well."The Old Man said and Grandpa nodded his head in agreement.

We picked up the parachute and put it in its bag and stored it with the helmet and gas mask, at the back of the workshop beside the tractor shed. And decided to call it a day, with George being the man of the moment.

A tractor race and more parachuting

A few weeks later, George and me were at a loose end. Grandpa, with Mum and Dad had gone to the market in Dumfries. Mum to do a bit of shopping and Grandpa and the Old Man to take some rabbits to the Butchers in the Venal and to see what price lambs were making in the livestock market. They wouldn't take us because they hadn't enough room in the Austin pickup with all rabbits in the back. So we decided to have a tractor race. Just to pass the time away.

Robert and Austin were coming up to play sometime later and Graham was also supposed to be coming up from Shieldhill and there's no doubt that a few more would hear about us having a tractor race and would appear.

We had got the wee grey Fergie tractor, the old Standard Ford and a David Brown crawler, that had tracks instead of wheels. George and me fired the old Standard Ford up, you had to start it on petrol and when it warmed up you switched over from petrol to paraffin and it would run like a Singer sewing machine. There was only one down-side with it, the clutch and brakes were on the same peddle but we weren't worried about things like that. George took it for a spin around the rickyard to get the feel of things and I thought I would take the crawler for a trial run just to see what that went like. Now when you drive a crawler it doesn't have a steering wheel just two levers that you pull to make it turn one way or the other. I pulled into the rick yard from the tractor shed and George bounced past on the old Standard Ford. I drew in behind him and opened the throttle up but the crawler wasn't made for the race track and the old Standard Ford was getting away from me at quite a speed. George was hanging on to the steering wheel for grim death whilst bouncing uncontrollably on the big springy iron seat.

The crawler's tracks were digging up the track round the rick yard and making a lot of noise and before you could say Jack Robinson, George was coming up again behind me. Well, I thought he would slow down behind me but I think, as usual, he was out of control, because when he came past me on the bottom bend, it looked like he was trying to grab the hand throttle to slow it down, but to no avail. The front wheel clipped a boulder and the tractor headed for the thick hawthorn hedge that surrounded the rick yard and nose dived half-way through it. As he hit the hedge and lurched through it, George flew forward and his hand hit the throttle and shut the revs down while his knee hit the gear lever, knocking it out of gear and stopping the tractor right in the middle of the hedge. He wasn't hurt and he was definitely glad it had stopped even if it was in the middle of the hedge.

I stopped the Crawler and went over to have a look and see what we could do to get the tractor out. It just sat there with the engine ticking over. George got back on it, put it in reverse and tried to drive out of the hedge but the front wheels were lodged over a large stump of wood and no matter what we did it wouldn't budge. So we decided to pull it out of the hedge with the crawler. We got the short wire rope that was hanging on the wall in the tractor shed, reversed the crawler up to the Standard Ford, drawbar to drawbar, put the hitch pins in and with George back on the tractor and me on the crawler with the lowest gear I could find, we started putting on the tension for the big pull. We thought it would be hard to get out of the hedge but once the tractor's front wheels were back over the stump, it just popped out like a cork out of a bottle.

As far as we could see, there was no damage to the tractor but the hedge was in need of a bit of repair. Austin and Bob turned up just then and we decided we would have to repair the hedge by blocking the hole up so that the Old Man wouldn't see the damage and also we had to cover up the tracks the crawler had made. We started to put the broken branches of the hedge back and tried to make it look as good as new and then we got the spade and rake and tried to smooth over the crawler tracks. When we finished we stood back to check to see if we had missed anything. George reckoned Davey Crocket himself, wouldn't find those tracks so we put the crawler back in the tractor shed.

It was there that Austin spotted the parachute hanging on the back wall and as we had decided not to do any more tractor racing, we started talking about what Barnsey had said, about his Uncle Angus, who was in the Para's during the war. He had said when they were training, they used to practice, by being towed behind a jeep, or a lorry.

"We could do that with the wee Grey Fergie." Bob said.

"Yeah that's a great idea," everyone agreed, "let's get the Fergie and we'll go into the Ley's and try it there." By this time, Grahame had come up from Shieldhill so we got the Fergie and headed off to the Ley's which was just at the back of the small farm wood.

Because George a couple of months ago had shown his prowess at airmanship and, presumably hadn't lost his touch, he was the chosen one, the one who was going to show us all how to do it. The one, who for the last couple of months, had been living on his remarkable acts and heroics. We got George harnessed up and got the big white African helmet on him ready for takeoff. The tractor was ready and we thought we were ready but had forgot about the tow rope. We hadn't got a tow rope. We hadn't got any rope long enough. It would have to be at least a hundred feet long and there were no ropes around here that long.   Everybody was really disappointed. That is everybody bar George, who, realizing he wouldn't have to show off his prowess, began to all of a sudden talk in a more brave and confident manner. He was just about to remove his harness, when Austin chirped in, saying that there was a half roll of binder twine in the tractor shed and that was nearly as strong as rope and it would be well long enough.

At this Bob and Graham ran back to the tractor shed to fetch the binder twine. When they arrived back with the twine, we measured out what we thought was about a hundred feet. George wasn't quite so chirpy now, as we tied the Binder twine to his harness and got him ready for flight. Once we got George sorted out, we turned the tractor into the wind and tied the binder twine onto the drawbar of the Tractor. I started to take up the slack with the tractor. We used the same system we had used up the hill, when George had made his amazing flight down from the old fort. Bob and Graham held the parachute out to catch the wind. I had promised not to go any faster than you could run and we had a fair head wind. In other words perfect flying conditions. Just then my brother John, turned up with Davey Marshal and Barnsey, to see what was happening.

I started off, slowly at first but gradually increasing my speed and when I looked back, George was airborne. He was shouting and squealing but so was everyone else, as they ran after us down the field. As I reached the bottom, I made a miscalculation. Instead of stopping and letting George float down to ground and land like a big bird, I turned ninety degrees and drove along the Spring Burn. When I looked back to see where George was, he was flying along beside me, because the wind had stiffened and it was blowing towards the farm. If it hadn't been for the mud guard, the binder twine would have wrapped around the back wheel and reeled George in. I shouted to him that I would head back towards the farm. He didn't reply and seemed more interested in keeping his big white desert helmet on, so I turned another ninety degrees and headed back towards the farm.

Everyone was running across the field trying to catch up with the action but when I turned towards the farm the wind seemed to get up and George was directly in front of the tractor, about thirty foot up and looking directly at me flying backwards. When I slowed down he went higher and when I went faster he got lower, so we ended up with the yoyo effect again but at least this time he was tethered. By this time the wood behind the farm was quickly advancing on us. It was decision time and everyone was shouting for me to stop, for some reason. That's when I saw the new electric wires that had been strung across the fields a couple of weeks ago and so I stopped. George drifted over the wires and thank God the wind dropped and he drifted towards the ground only to be held up by the overhead cables and binder twine.

The gang by this time had caught up with us and grabbed the parachute in case the wind got up again. George was hanging about ten foot up looking like a future Mayoral candidate for Shieldhill or even Dumfries, with his white desert helmet still intact and within touching distance of safety. We let him dangle while we discussed how to get him down. Barnsey said,

"I'll cut the binder twine, that'll get him down," and he started to get his penknife out but by that time I had driven the tractor slowly forward, lowering him down. Just before he put his feet on the ground, the binder twine broke and the little jolt was just enough to dislodge his big white desert helmet, which spun round like a top when it hit the ground. They had all been shouting because they didn't know that the electricity hadn't yet been connected. Barnsey said.

"If that had been connected and had live wires, George would have been chips. Fried chips."

Just then, the Old Man appeared at the rick yard gate and wasn't too happy at what he had just witnessed. When they had arrived back from the market in Dumfries, Aunty May had said, I think them boys are up to something, because I've heard the tractors running and all sorts of shouting and squealing from the back of the barn and down the field. George was just getting out of the parachute harness, when the Old Man struck and gave me and George a bloody good slapping and by God he could slap.

I was crying but George wasn't, he wouldn't cry for anything. It was his way of saying,

"I'm small but I won't show anyone weakness." Complete defiance. By the time the Old Man had finished with us, everyone else had disappeared and Barnsey was taking the tractor back to the tractor shed and getting out of the way. The old bugger then got the parachute and threw it on the rubbish dump at the end of the wood and set it alight with a splash of paraffin and we had to stand there and watch as our favorite plaything went up in smoke. But he didn't burn the helmet or gas mask. At dinner that night, he pulled out a letter from the Scottish Electricity Board and read it out to everybody round the table. It went as follows,

'No one should ever attempt to touch wires or transformer boxes in any circumstances. Doing so could end up in instant death.' The Old Man went on to say,

"Tell your mates that means climbing electric poles, flying kites and parachuting."

After reading out the letter, we got a lecture on how lucky we had been that the power had not yet been connected. Grandpa nodded his head in agreement.

"Oh! By the way." The Old Man added, "While walking round the rick yard, I noticed that there was a hole in the hedge and the old Standard Ford has got grass sticking out of the rim of its front tyre. But it was getting too dark to see properly. I'll have a closer look tomorrow. You two can get to your beds right now and take heed of what's been said." Aunty May chirped in.

"Yes you boys. Up the golden stairs right now," with a little giggle.

Going up the stairs I said to George,

"The Old Man's a better tracker than what we thought." George replied,

"At least as good as Davey Crocket."

Electricity and the steamer

Electricity had finally reached the farm but wouldn't get connected for a few weeks yet. Not until they had put the transformer onto the twin poles at the edge of the paddock, and connected it onto a master box in the dairy. Things were starting to take shape now. The new byre and dairy were nearly ready. They just had to put the big sliding doors on and finish off the roof. The electricians were running wires all over the byre and dairy and on to the house as well. Ready for when we got connected up to the mains.

When the electricity finally got connected, we had an abundance of new fangled things to play with. Every room in the house had an electric bulb hanging from the middle of the ceiling and you switched them on with a dark brown Bakelite switch just beside the door. The new byre had three electric light bulbs hanging from the roof and in the dark you could see better than you could with half a dozen Tilley lamps. There was a light in the dairy too and milk cooler and three new milking machines, all worked by a suction pump and in the corner sat a big chest called a steamer.

We were definitely moving with the times. We had a new byre and dairy and ten more cows. That made twenty six now. And no more hand milking. A new tractor, the wee grey Fergie and mechanical clippers for shearing the sheep. But biggest thing of all was electricity. No more Tilley lamps and wee oil lamps to go to bed with. We had a new electric wireless that didn't need a battery charged and changed every week.

A few of us were standing about one day, looking for something to do and we just happened to be at the door to the dairy and Austin was switching the light on and off, trying to understand how it could react so quickly. We then started to look around the dairy and the new fangled things that were in it. There was the new milk cooler making a slight burring noise and then there was the milking machine pump and a big steel sink for general washing and in the corner was a great big chest, about six feet by four and it was standing on its own legs. This was the steamer, or sterilizer. When you had finished doing the milking, everything that had come into contact with milk had to be sterilized and was put in this machine for fifteen minutes or so, till everything was spotlessly clean.

We were all looking at the new gear, especially the steamer, when somebody wondered what it might be like to be inside it whilst it was on. A volunteer was asked for but no one came forward. So we picked one. It was George, the school mistress's son, who we reckoned was the one who most needed a wash. We finally got George into the steamer, with a bit of friendly persuasion and promising to let him out on demand. He got in and looked quite comfortable as we closed the door and locked the cantilever handles ready for the steam. There was no way out for George but we had promised to free him on request. There were just a couple of drip holes to let water out of the bottom. My brother John started up the steamer which used to take about five minutes to get going and warm up.

We all stood around watching to see what would happen. After about five minutes, a little bit of steam started to come out of drip hole in the floor of the steamer. But George seemed to be quiet happy, or so his muffled voice implied. About a minute later there seemed to be a slight sense of urgency in his muffled voice and someone thought they heard him say he wanted out but we thought he could stand a bit more yet. But George realizing his predicament, started to kick and bang the sides of the steamer and by this time the steam was coming out a lot quicker and soon the banging was reaching a crescendo and nobody wanted to open the door in case George went for their throat and killed them. Brother John shut off the steam and opened the door of the steamer. Everyone ran for the doors and windows in case George went wild, ready for a quick getaway but there was no need .George slithered out onto the dairy floor, steaming slightly. A bit like a calf being born. He lay there gradually coming to his senses.

On seeing he wasn't going to kill anybody, we all started coming back. He was totally saturated and with his eyes getting used to the day light, we gradually got him into the sun and found an old empty hessian sack to dry him off with. Do you know that was the cleanest anybody had ever seen George and his hair was really blond!

Horace at Christmas

About two weeks before Christmas, Dad used to buy a good turkey from the market. It was usually about 18 to 20lbs and would have to be fed until a few days before Christmas. The Christmas of 1952 was no different but for one thing. I, at the grand old age of eight, had the turkey put in my charge. I had to do the feeding and watering, making sure it was 'OK' for Christmas dinner. We had an empty hen house, so I picked up the turkey, which was in an old Hessian sack with just his head popping out and took him there. Mum said

"Mind you don't let anything happen to it boy." Aunty May echoed her words.

"Aye, don't let anything happen to it boy. Christmas would'na be Christmas without a turkey would it?" I settled the turkey down in the hen house, watered and fed him, making sure the sneck was on the door, saying goodnight to him as I left.

"Real responsible job." I muttered to myself as I walked back to the house.

After a couple of days of feeding it, it got used to me and was like a pet. It knew feeding time and popped its head out and started cackling when it heard me coming. Just like a pet. I named him Horace. I didn't know whether it was a boy or girl but it looked like a Horace to me. Over the next few days, Horace and me got quite matey. He would eat out of my hand and follow me around the yard. So I got quite a shock when Dad told me not to feed him anymore, because he didn't want his pallet and gut full of corn when they gutted him. I had forgotten the reason he was here and had got too friendly with my charge. I was horrified.

A couple of days before Christmas, Dad told Barnsey the herdsman and my brother John to go and do the dastardly deed and prepare him for the oven. I didn't know what to do. They went and got Horace out of the hen house and, ignoring my protests, took him into the barn where there was a light. I followed blubbing my eyes out.

Barnsey had Horace by the legs upside down holding him at arm's length. John was going to whack him round the head with a big stick. I was whimpering at the barn door. John addressed the stick to Horace's head. Barnsey was calling on John to hurry up. Horace was looking at me upside down. I am sure he cried for help. My brother's swing was imminent. You could see he was going to give it a real belter. I turned the light off.

In the dark all hell let loose. Lots and lots of shouting. Lots and lots of flapping and bawling. I switched the lights back on. Barnsey was reeling about on the floor holding his legs. Pain etched on his face. Horace was sitting on a beam up in the barn roof. John was standing there with the stick, wondering what had happened. But not for long.

"You bloody stupid boy," he yelled, throwing the stick which hit me round the legs, smashing a torch in my pocket. He caught hold of me and gave me a really good smacking. They then went back into the barn. Horace wasn't so lucky this time. The next time I saw Horace, he was hanging upside down in the dairy, fully plucked, ready for the oven. Barnsey couldn't milk the cows because of his leg and Dad and John had to do the milking. I wasn't very popular.

On Christmas Eve I had to go to bed early.

"Off to bed with you now" Mum said, handing me my clay piggy hot water bottle. "Aye."" up the golden stairs," said Aunt May with a little giggle, giving me a slap on the bum as I walked past, at the bottom of the stairs. Sandy the cat was lying on my bed when I got into it, purring loudly and I soon cried myself to sleep.

When I woke my hot water bottle was cold so I put it out beside the bed being careful to get my hands back in the warmth quickly. Then I realized,

"It's Christmas." I soon forgot about the cold, jumping out of bed to see what was in my sock. Sure enough there was an orange and apple and a brown paper bag full of peanuts also two wee brown parcels. I ripped them open. Underpants. Socks. I love the smell of new things. I heard someone speaking downstairs. I listened real hard.

"It's sna'in, it's sna'in." I could hear Aunty May saying. I leaped up, got dressed quickly and ran downstairs to put my clogs on.

"'Take yer time boy" shouted Aunty May as I ran out of the back kitchen door and into the yard. The flakes were big and fluffy falling silently to the ground which was covered with a thick white blanket. White everywhere. I stamped around making and kept falling over. Aunty May and Mum were laughing their heads off at the kitchen door. The dogs were going mad, chasing each other, chasing their tails and riffling their noses through the snowflakes and snorting. There were paw marks and pee marks and hens cackling loudly. A robin was hopping about all fluffed up.

I went to the byre. The cows unsettled themselves in anticipation of being fed. I broke a bale of hay. The smell of dried grass seeds and pollen. It hit you straight away. A breath of summer on Christmas Day.

The old cows swung their heads from side to side giving you a look with a wild eye, heads straining in their yokes, licking their noses with raspy tongues till they got their hay.

Excitement was limited in our Christmas festivities. It mattered. But other things mattered more. You did your chores. Made sure the animals were fed and watered and lagged pipes against the frost. Only when that had been done, could you indulge in Christmas fare. It was the one day of the year that we all got washed and changed for dinner. We all began to take our seats at the large wooden table in the back kitchen. Barnsey hobbled in. The Aga glowed with heat. It was covered with pots and pans full of Christmas fare.

And in the oven was Horace.

The Moffat pig

It was Sunday morning and we were all having breakfast after feeding and milking the cows. The Old Man said he had seen a farmer from Moffat in the market at Dumfries that had a litter of pigs for sale and he was going up to Moffat to see them and buy them if they were ok. He said me and George could go with him if we wanted to. We were all for it. We were leaving just before half past nine and Dad said we would be back for dinner.

The old Austin pickup had a canvas cover over it. With the canvas back on either side we had a good view out of the back. We took two bales of straw and a couple of hessian sacks with us to put the piglets in if we bought them. We had never been to Moffat before and were quite excited as we sat in the back bouncing along and looking at the Scottish country side rolling past.

After about three quarters of an hour we were going over a bridge where years ago some doctor had murdered his Mrs, chopped her up, wrapped the bits up in brown paper and threw the parts over the bridge into the river, thinking they would disappear. But they didn't. A while later a chap doing a bit of fly fishing, hooked a leg a leg. They hung the doctor. After that it was called the doctor's bridge.

We finally got onto the road that went to the Moffat farmer's farm and he was waiting at the gate to meet us. Dad and the old farmer had a good old chat and George and me stretched our legs and loosened up. Maybe Dad should have loosened up too.

The piglets were in the middle of the paddock in a corrugated tin shelter with their mother the old sow Dad climbed over the five bar gate, saying he was going to have a look at them and see if they were worth the money the farmer was asking for. They weren't quite so chatty when it concerned money. The old pig farmer shouted after him to watch out for the old sow Dad said he was ok and strode out towards the sty. We stood at the gate looking through the bars at the Old Man approaching the corrugated tin shelter. It was about fifty yards away from the gate. The old farmer kept on saying,

"Watch that old sow Tom."

"It'll be ok," he said, picking one of the piglets up from inside the shelter. That's when it happened. An eruption of pig. A big Mummy pig that wasn't too happy about Dad handling her baby pig. Well as luck would have it, he had a head start, about five yards to be precise. Well I've seen men run and I've seen fear. But I've never seen a man running in fear of his life before. We hadn't got time to open the gate and he went over the five barred gate barely touching it escaping by the seat of his pants as the old sow hit the gate so hard, it broke one of the cross spars on it.

"I told you to watch that old pig, Tom," The old farmer said.

"What the hell are you feeding it on," the Old Man replied. Anyway, I think the spirit the old sow had shown impressed Dad and he struck a deal with the Moffat pig farmer for the piglets. Then all we had to do was separate the piglets from the sow. George and me did not volunteer. There was a keep pen in the corner of the paddock and the old sow went in after some food that had been put down for her. We shut the gate, tying it with a bit of binder twine. Just in case. Keeping them as quiet as possible, we put the litter into the hessian sacks and put them in the back of the old Austin, in between the bales of straw. We then bade farewell to the old Moffat farmer and the Moffat Pig.

George and me made sure the piglets were ok in the back of the truck and we were home in no time. The piglets were put in a small shed full of straw behind the coal house to settle down.

Then it was dinner time when we told everybody about Dad's lucky escape. He said there was no luck in it at all. He was just teasing it and using himself as bait to get it away from the piglets.

George said,

"It certainly worked and the Moffat Pig nearly took the bait."

Barnsey in the byre

In the Byre the glass panes were small and of a poor quality with slight air bubbles and small defects. One had been removed recently and it looked like the putty had been put in by fingers and thumbs. There was a spider's web with a fat bellied owner standing watch. It scampered down a bolt hole at the presence of my breath as I closed in on the glass to get a closer look. I rubbed some dust from the glass and put my eyes right up to it and gazed through. It was getting dark and soon he would have to put the lights on. I had just got back from school and was determined to get my own back on Barnsey whose real name was Philip Barns, the herdsman.

My mind had been warped thinking of ways to get my revenge since Barnsey and my brother John ganged up on me and threw me in the sheep dip. This was in full sight and with the blessing of my Dad, who said I had got my just desserts and should not be so lippy. I rubbed the glass again and after a couple of minutes the lights were switched on. There were about twenty cows tied up in the byre all switching their tails and munching on their milking time feed. The milking machines quietly ticked. There were four units, two on either side and Barnsey in the middle completely unaware of the prying eyes.

I watched him for several minutes working away, gradually getting closer to the newly calved cows and heifers that would be milked last because of the richness of their milk. The heifers were more nervous than the older cows and did not like the machines. He was trying to get the machine cups on one of the heifer's teats when I struck. A well aimed chunk of cow cake hit the heifer on the rear end as he was putting the units on. Even I didn't expect what happened next. The heifer kicked Barnsey and the units right across the byre. I thought it had killed him. I stood motionless for a second. It was a second too long. He spotted me and in a real rage started after me. I ran like mad being chased by a madman. I wondered if I had over done it. He caught me in seconds and beat me half senseless. I was crying and really frightened as he took me by the scruff of the neck and dragged me back into the byre in a blind rage, marched me up to one of the old cows that had just calved, lifted up its tail and stuck my head straight up its backside and rubbed my nose and face in all the muck and afterbirth for what seemed like an eternity.

We laugh about it now but at the time, I wished I had gone home and done my homework and not peered through the window.

The BRM Racer (Barnsey's Racing Motor)

George and me were playing up and down the back yard with an old pram we had found, when looking for hens nests in an old out house. Old Nell the collie was joining in and barking because of the squeaky noises it was making as it bounced along the cobbled back yard. Barnsey the herdsman came out of the byre to see what all the noise was about and when he saw what we had, he said that he had made a kart out of an old pram when he was young and he would give us a hand to make one.

So after he finished the milking and we had finished our tea, we got started on making our go kart. Everybody got involved. The nights were drawing out and it didn't get dark till later, so the first night we had got the wheels and axles off the pram and started making the frame of the cart. We got an old tin drum for the feet of the driver and built a cockpit with the base and cradle of the old pram. It was beginning to take shape. George and me thought it was beginning to look good.

Mum and Aunty May said it was getting late and it was time for bed.

The next day after school we got going again and after tea Barnsey and Brother John came to help. We had bolts, nuts and washers everywhere. Barnsey seemed to know what he was doing. It started looking really good. It was steered with a rope off each side of the front axle and lots of folks were getting interested in it. We stood back admiring our work. There was something missing.

"It needs painting." Barnsey said. We all agreed. Dad said he had a can of green paint in the tractor shed. We went and got it and prized the lid open with a screwdriver. It needed mixing up, so we took the skin off it with the screwdriver and mixed it up with a stick. It only took a minute or two. Barnsey said it was British Racing Green, so that was ideal.

They allowed George and me to paint it. After all it was our cart. We soon had it painted and about everything else in the immediate area as well as on George and me. I think we had more paint on us than there was on the cart. Aunty May wasn't too happy about the state we were in and made us stay outside until we got cleaned up. There's nothing like the smell of paraffin while eating your dinner.

After we finished our grub, we pulled the cart out of the barn to show Mum and Aunty May. The paint was still wet so we couldn't ride in it or try it out but we just wanted to show it off to everybody. There was a real sense of achievement in the air. Everyone seemed impressed. The only thing left to do was paint the name on it. Mum had a small tin of white paint and one of Aunty Ena's small paint brushes and Barnsey started to paint the name on the sides. It looked right impressive.

The BRM. The best kart in the South of Scotland. Barnsey's Racing Motor. It had to be the best cart ever. It was decided to give it its test run down the Bray the next day after tea. When it was time for the test run everybody was there. It seemed like the half of Dumfrieshire had heard about it and all our mates from school were there too. Even Jimmy Little was there with his travelling shop. Ronnie Shuttleworth from Bruntshields was there and the Old Man.

Barnsey said me and George were too young to do the test run and that Brother John should do it, because he was older and a lot stronger.

"He's thirteen and you're only nine." He said.

So reluctantly we agreed and it was decided to start from the catchment area of the sheep dip and head off down the Bray towards Shieldhill. At the bottom of the Bray there was a slight bend over the burn and then it flattened off for a bit, then it was slightly uphill and after that it was downhill all the way to the river. About a mile or so.

John was all ready to go. All he needed was a good push to get him started and he was away, slowly at first but soon we couldn't keep up with him. Even the dogs couldn't keep up with him. He was really going for it. Approaching the bend at the bottom of the Bray, he disappeared altogether. There was a muffled shout and lots of howling and bawling coming from the bottom of the Bray, in amongst the brambles and bushes along the side of the burn. Everybody started running down the road to see what had happened. I'd like to say the brakes had malfunctioned. But it didn't have any because we were relying on gravity on the uphill bit of road to stop the cart. It hadn't made it that far. But John was lucky for when he came off the road, he went straight into the ferns and brambles and they stopped him from going into the burn. And apart from a few scratches and grazes he was OK. The BRM was completely unrepairable and was left where it had come to rest.

Everybody walked back to the farm saying how brave John was. Mum and Aunty May put loads of lotion on John's cuts and scratches. Jimmy Little did a roaring trade with his mobile shop.

The BRM had crashed on its maiden run. All that work up in smoke. Barnsey said he should have put some brakes on it. George said,

"Sometimes it pays to be too young and not strong enough."

"You might be right. I replied."

The Rolly-polly Club

After school George and me went up to the top of the hill to see Barnsey and Sandy who were fencing a flat bit of the hill up near the new Survey Post. When we got there, they were just about to pack up to go down to the farm and do the milking and feed the beasts. They jumped on the wee Fergie and Bogie trailer and headed off leaving George and me mucking about. What on Earth could we get up to up here.

After a few minutes we had had enough of pelting stones at fence posts, when George noticed the new Survey Post which was about a hundred yards away at the very top of the hill. So we decided to go and investigate.

Sandy had left his old herding stick leaning on a fence post and George picked it up as we walked past, kidding on it was a golf club by hitting the odd stone and bits of sheep shite as we walked up to the Post. When we got there it wasn't a post. It was made with concrete, wide at the bottom and a bit narrower at the top. A sort of pyramid thing, about four feet high, with a brass plate, really well embedded in the concrete top. It had three screw holes in it to attach measuring things to. George climbed on top of it, taking Sandy's stick with him. He stood and standing on top, swinging it around like a sword daring me to come anywhere near, while shouting and singing

"I'm the King of the Castle and you're the dirty wee Rascal. Every time I went near him, I got whacked, so it was time to do some thinking. I just had to knock him of his perch. It was then I happened to step on some sheep shite. It was an act of Go. My Prayers had been answered. I all of a sudden had the advantage.

Loads of sheep shite and George in his Castle, or should I say, very small plinth, didn't have any at all. He watched me carefully wondering what I was doing as I collected it up into a couple of heaps and then from a safe place just out of stick distance I launched my attack. A bit of a David and Goliath sort of thing, only I didn't have a sling but I plenty of sheep shite. I started with one shot at a time but when I saw I was getting on top of him with no return fire, I let him have it. Handfuls, double handfuls and finally he lost his stick and his balance and that was that. He was no longer the King of the Castle. He was now the dirty wee Rascal. Very dirty.

I then gave George a hand to get cleaned up. He wasn't too bad because a lot of the ammo was old and dry but there were a few wet ones. George being George, got one and hit me right in the middle of the forehead with it. He just had to have the last say.

Afterwards we wandered back down to where the men had been fencing, taking Sandy's stick with us. There was a heap of fence posts, wire strainers, spades, sledge hammers and rolls of barbed and plane wire. Nobody would touch anything up here, would they?

The barbed wire was in a small round ball and weighed about half a hundred weight. There was a hole in the middle of the roll, so you could put a stick through it and two of you could pick it up and walk along unwinding the barbed wire. We had a stick. We had Sandy's stick. We got a roll of barbed wire, stuck Sandy's stick through the middle and walked around to see what it was like carrying it and when we stopped, we were right on the edge of the steep hill and could see all the way down to the Connells farm and then as far as the railway line, on the way to the Hislop's farm. We just wondered, it's funny how George and me wondered about the same thing, at exactly the same time. What we wondered was how far the barbed wire would roll if we pushed it over the edge of the hill. We sent it over and away it went until it was completely out of sight. We last saw a couple of glints of sun. We reckoned by that time it was past the Connells and on its way to the Hislop's and the railway line.

We reckoned it was doing a hundred miles an hour. Maybe more and bouncing fifty feet in the air. We just had to have another go. So we went back to the heap of wire to get another roll but this time we got a roll of smooth wire. They were a lot bigger about the size of a car tyre but with no barbs. We rolled it to the edge and lined it up ready for the launch and it was off. We stood there amazed at the speed it was going and the height that it was bouncing and then it was gone. Just like the barbed wire, the occasional glint in the far, far distance, then nothing. It was real good fun but we thought better of doing any more.

Over the next few weeks we occasionally looked for those two rolls but we never did see them again. When we were down by the railway line we looked over the bridge for them. A train came along and we got blasted by the smoke. That was good fun, we loved the smell of smoke. But no wire rolls.

The rolls of wire were never mentioned. I don't think they missed them and when they ran out of wire, must have thought they had measured it up wrong.

We kept Mum and Aunty May.

Man Mountain Benny

Dad was so pleased with the way things were going, he said he would take Barnsey and Sandy Carson, to the wrestling at the Drill Hall in Dumfries, They were all for it, because they didn't get out much. They were acting like a couple of kids and doing wrestling in the middle of the backyard. Dad had rang up Willey Richardson to join them there, saying he would pay for the tickets. It wasn't starting till eight o clock but they had arranged to meet in the pub they used when they were at the market to have a few drinks before the wrestling started.

George and me had to go to bed at half past nine as it got dark. We were completely done in and were fast asleep in minutes. In our sleep, it must have been about eleven o'clock, I drowsily remember hearing Aunty May screeching with laughter before falling into a deep sleep again. The morning seemed to be upon us in the blink of an eye and breakfast was at eight and everyone was still laughing and giggling. It was over the breakfast table that George and me would eventually find out what all the giggling was about.

Apparently when they got to the Drill Hall, Dad got front row seats so they would get a better view of the ring and as the evening went on the crowd were getting quite boisterous, because, as Barnsey said,

"The fights so far, were a bit hairy fairy and weren't going down too well with the crowd and there was an uneasy feeling going around the Hall." But then it was the main bout of the evening which promised to liven things up.

It was Man Mountain Benny, a notoriously dirty fighter, versus "Razor Stitch-that-Jimmy Ruddock" whom they reckoned, carried a cut throat razor in the front flap of his cloth cap and had been responsible for quite a few scared faces and sliced ears around the Paisley area from where he hailed. The fight got under way and the Man Mountain was definitely getting on top of Razor Ruddock, all be it by using really dirty moves and eye gouging. But the Razor was getting back in the picture and in a Herculean effort threw the Man Mountain right across the ring, through the ropes. He fell on the floor right in front of Dad and Willey.

As he got on his hands and knees to get up, facing the stage with an evil look for Razor Ruddock in his twisted eyes, my Old Man got off his seat and planted a well aimed brown leather brogue right up Benny's arse, calling him a dirty bastard as he did so.

Well the Man Mountain lurched forwards, slightly off balance and ended up with his head stuck in the curtain drapes that encircled the bottom of the ring and the Old Man retook his seat next to Willey.

When Benny finally got his head out of the drapes, he turned round bellowing,

"Who the hell did that," and looking back at the crowd in the general direction of our lot with real malice written all over his face. Dad pointed at Willey who was immediately stricken with fear and on looking at Man Mountain Benny, vacated his seat and was jumping rows of seats before making for the isle and the exit door, to roars of laughter from the audience.

The wrestling recommenced and Man Mountain Benny finally conquered Razor Ruddock by lying on top of him for a count of three and afterwards he wouldn't get off him and nearly smothered him. But the laugh of the night was Willey hurdling over the seats and running up the aisle and out of the door of the Drill Hall. Everybody thought they had had a great night. Even Willy. Eventually.

The Coronation

With the big day fast approaching, we were getting ready for it. *June the second, nineteen fifty three.* Coronation day.

We had one of the highest hills for miles around and had to have a big bonfire on the top of it beside the survey plinth as a beacon the night of the Coronation. Apparently they were doing it all over the country at the same time. So everybody was bringing all their rubbish from the neighboring farms and dumping it in the paddock. Barnsey and Sandy Carson were taking it up to the top of the hill with the wee grey Fergie and the bogie trailer and building a great big bonfire. Me and George thought it would be the biggest bonfire in the south of

Scotland. Barnsey said they will probably be able to see this in England when it gets going. We all nodded our heads in agreement and looked towards the Solway and onwards to England. Going up and down with loads of stuff to burn on the bonfire, Barnsey and Sandy made sure they didn't take any short cuts. After seeing what had happened to the Old Man, with the old Standard Ford, they were definitely sticking to the not so steep parts and the old Roman road and not taking any risks.

The Old Man had decided to get a television installed for the Coronation and was getting it from an old mate called Willie Richardson, who came from Castle Douglas. He was going to fix the aerial to the chimney and tune it to the nearest transmitter. Wherever that was. As of yet it wasn't an exact science. On the Saturday morning Willie arrived with the television, the aerial and all the wires and fixings for attaching it to the chimney stack. He said things were looking up and he was really busy with the run up to the Coronation.

"Everybody wants one, not today or tomorrow, faster than that, they want it yesterday." He said, grinning like a cat, as he got out of his brand new Morris Minor van, with a brand new double extending ladder strapped to its roof. Dad came up to the house from the byre when he heard Willie arrive. They were real good mates and were always messing about when they got together and with the new television they were like two kids with a new toy.

After having a quick look at what Willie had got in the back of the van and what he was getting for his money. The Old Man and Willie decided to have a cup of tea and a couple of buttered scones before starting on the serious job of installing the bloody thing.

"Can't work on an empty stomach, can we boys." Willie said, as they went through the back kitchen door. Me and George nodding in agreement as we walked in behind them. Willie greeted Mum and Aunty May like long lost friends, and picked up a scone as he sat down to have his tea. The women were looking on for his approval of their home baked scones and Willie knew how to show his approval as he golloped up loads of them.

After about three-quarters of an hour, teatime was over and it was time to get to work and install the new aerial and television. We were told to keep out of the way as Willie adjusted his ladders and leant them against the rhones, before going up to the top of the ladders and tying them secure on an existing bracket, so as they wouldn't slip. George and me climbed up into our tree hut and we were nearly as high as the chimney that Willie was working on and could see everything he was doing. Willie climbed up the lead gulley, with the Old Man standing on the top of the ladder handing him the wires and brackets that he needed. And a bit of encouragement too. After about an hour Willie had fitted the aerial and dropped a long wire down from it, to the front room window. Once he had connected the wire to the television he would be ready to tune it in to the transmitter. The Old Man wanted to have it near the fire in the front room, so that we could all sit round and watch it and keep warm at the same time.

"And in the winter we could toast bread on the fire with the toasting fork." George piped in as we all stood there looking into the corner, on the left hand side of the fireplace, where the television would finally rest.

"Come on you boys, go and play outside and keep out of the way and let the man get on with his work, it's all fiddly now, with wires and plugs and things." The Old Man said. Willie got out a bag of screwdrivers and pliers and started trimming the wire with his pocket knife.

George and me went out into the yard and were wondering what to do. We heard Chips the terrier going mad yelping and barking down the back of the barn, so we ran down the yard to see what he had found. Sure enough he had got a rat or something trapped under a pile of wood and old railway sleepers. They were far too heavy for George and me to lift but Chips was going mad, so there was definitely something there. We decided to go and get one of the ferrets, so we went and got Fred, he seemed the liveliest and most up to the job. We didn't bother to stick him in the hessian sack, we used to carry them around in, because it was just a short distance back to the sleepers and Chips was still going mad, barking and yelping and fruitlessly gnawing the end of a sleeper.

With all the noise and commotion going on with Chips, Fred the ferret was biting at the bit and squirming so I threw him down at the end of the railway sleepers and stood back with George. With were both of us firmly grabbing our sticks. We assumed action stations and prepared for Battle. Old Fred had a sniff at the end of the sleepers and stuck his head in for a look to see what was what. His old tail started shaking and he was gone down the back of the sleepers and pile of old wood with Chips at the other end. With George on one flank and me on the other, what could go wrong?

Just at that moment Barnsey and old Nell, who had been checking the sheep at the back of the hill, walked into the yard. There was a lot of movement in amongst the wood pile and the rat jumped out but on seeing Chips, jumped straight back into the wood pile. Fred was still in there and it was just about three seconds before it reappeared, this time from the middle of the woodpile. Sensing a need for more urgency it decided to make for the weakest part of its encirclement which was me and my trusty stick. I took a good swing at my target. I hated rats. We all hated rats, Fred the Ferret, Chips the Terrier, George. Everybody hated rats. My swing had perfect timing but not as perfect as old Nell's who on seeing what was happening, seized the opportunity to get in first. As the rat ran right into old Nell's mouth, my trusty stick hit old Nell's head. I don't know where but, the way she went down, probably between the eyes.

The rat not believing its luck made a beeline for the midden, with Chips and Fred the Ferret and George in close pursuit but ratty had beat them to it and scarpered up the drain that led up to the byre and loose boxes. Old Fred and Chips had lost the chase. Old Nell just lay there motionless. Then everybody gathered around to see if she was dead. Barnsey was there in a jiffy, to assess the situation. It looked bad for Nell, as she lay there motionless.

We all stood back to let Barnsey have a look and as he knelt down to try to revive her, there was a twitch and he gave her a rub behind the head. An eye opened and Barnsey started massaging her round her back as well and George and me helped rubbing her head and paws, to get the circulation going and after a few minutes she was back on her feet, albeit a bit groggily.

George then got Fred, who was running around the Midden looking for ratty and stuck him back in the hutch. We all then went back to see what Willy and the Old Man were up to. Willy had got all the wires and things connected up and now all that had to be done, was tune it in. It was making squeaky sort of noises and the screen was grey with lots of sparks and white dots on it. Willy and the Old Man weren't worried about Old Nell. They were too engrossed in their new toy. Willy said, if he sets it up about right, he should get a picture of a test card on the screen to help him tune it.

"There're no programme's on until later." He moaned.

"I'll have to go up to the chimney and point the aerial and get it smack onto the transmitter to get the best picture. We'll have to form a chain to shout the directions where you want me to point the aerial" Willy said. "Tom can watch the Television, you boys can shout the instructions through the house to Barnsey, who can stand at the top of the ladder and shout the instructions to me up at the top of the chimney and I'll adjust the aerial." Willy said, he looking pleased and slightly smug with his efforts. It was obviously going well, so far anyway.

Willy got in his position on top of the chimney with his adjustable spanner at the ready to tighten the bolts on the aerial when the right picture came into Dad's view. We all assumed our positions and the Old Man shouted left a bit and I shouted to George, left a bit. George shouted up the ladder to Barnsey who relayed it on to Willy, who promptly said,

"A big bit or a small bit."

In the end the up directions and the down directions, were going at a fair old pace and it was just a matter of time before it was a great big muddle. Even Old Nell who was sitting at the back door watching the mayhem going on must have thought,

"I've come back from the dead and now this."

Just then Willy dropped his adjustable spanner straight down the chimney. The one that went down to the front room, taking a load of soot from the inside, of the yet to be swept chimney and depositing it on the hearth and quite a bit of the front room. Willy looked down the chimney flue to see where his adjustable spanner had gone and heard a wailing noise come back up the chimney from the Old Man about the mess. On hearing this Willy thought the best thing to do, was for Dad to shout up the chimney and cut out the middle men and boys. After about half an hour Willy let out a yelp, a sort of shout of joy. A decent picture had finally been obtained. The Old Man came out of the back door looking pleased with himself, although covered in soot. Willy started down from the roof, untying the ladders from the Rhone bracket as he descended to ground level. We all then made our way to the front room to look at a television for the very first time. There was nothing on, just the test card and all grey, with the odd spark. Old Nell stood at the door of the sooty lounge, looking at us, looking at it, wondering what it was.

Just then Aunty May shouted from the back kitchen that the dinner was ready and she was just ladling the soup at the table and to hurry up and get it before it gets cold.

"Come on now, right away." she said.

We all started heading for the kitchen and dinner. We were all clean except the Old Man, who must have thought he had the best job of all, just watching the screen and shouting orders but ended up all covered in soot. Mum made him wash outside at the spicket before he could sit down for dinner. Willy as usual, eat his soup with gusto and complimented the women folk on their cooking. Also asking for another helping, with Aunty May obliging right away, with her ladle always at the ready.

"Aye there's always plenty of soup in this pot Willy." Aunty May said.

Old Nell sat at the back kitchen door and wagged her tail, seemingly none the worse, after her near death experience. Willy, having dined well and having completed yet another successful installation, was soon making his way back to Castle Douglas. We didn't realize it at the time but that little machine in the front room would gradually change everyone's lives, even Mum and the Old Man would become addicted to it eventually.

That first night we all watched it until it finished and it must have been getting on for ten o' clock when the National Anthem come on and Dad stood up and we all stood up and sang. Dad then switched it off and we all stood there watching a white dot in the middle of the screen, gradually disappearing. No one moved until it had finally gone and disappeared into a grey nothingness.

The old folks went into the back kitchen to have a cup of tea before going to bed, being slightly bemused with their first initiation of the new media of Television. George and me went to bed and to tell you the truth, we were slightly bemused too. We could catch rabbits and find birds' nests, even ones that aren't in the bird book' but we couldn't work out how the hell you could get pictures out of thin air.

On the Monday morning of June the 1st, at school we all got presented with a Coronation Mug, all nine of us. I think Mrs. Leven, the school mistress, presented herself with one as well. The next day was the big day. Coronation Day June the 2nd 1953. Tuesday morning arrived and everybody was up and doing their work and chores early because the Coronation was due to start at 11am sharp and nobody wanted to miss anything, especially the crowning.

We had Breakfast early and Barnsey had finished the milking early so as to get ready as he and Sandy were in charge of lighting the bonfire on top of the hill after ten that night. They were going to use a gallon of paraffin and a dry bale of straw.

The women folks were baking scones, cakes, shortbread and all sorts of things, ready for the multitude that were due to come to the celebration and it was due to start at 11 o' clock.

The Old Man had got a load of fireworks when he went to the market in Dumfries on Saturday and when he came home he brought them into the back kitchen to show everyone. We were told in no uncertain terms, not to go anywhere near them or we would get more than a good hiding. We would get a severe thrashing. George looked at me and we went out into the back yard to play, with the Old Man shouting to us as we went out of the door that he wasn't joking. That was on the Saturday night and since then we had looked everywhere for them but we still had not found them. We just wanted to have a look at them and smell the gunpowder and look at the boxes and pictures on them.

George and me searched every nook and cranny. We looked in the cowshed and in the barn, the rick yard, the dairy, under the Old Man and Mums bed, Aunty Mays bed, Barnsey's bed, the dogs kennel, the pigs sty, absolutely everywhere but we still could not find them because we eventually found out that he had given them to Bob Telfer for safe keeping until the big day.

Folks started arriving from early on and a party atmosphere soon started to develop. Most of the men folks brought crates of beer and some of them brought whisky too. The Old Man told Barnsey and Sandy Carson, to steady on with the booze, because they still had to do the milking and feed the beasts, plus light the bonfire at ten o'clock tonight.

It was a long day and the celebrations began to develop their own atmosphere, with people coming and going and surging towards the front room when they heard a sudden roar from the stalwarts, mostly women, who had ensconced themselves in front of the new Ferguson nine inch Television. They knew that if they left they might miss something, as there were no instant replays back then. George and me popped in and had a look now and then but it seemed to go on forever and it got a bit boring. We couldn't wait for the fireworks and bonfire at ten. That should be real fun. Some of the folks from the neighboring farms went back in the afternoon, to feed their beasts and do the milking but they would be back later on for the bonfire and fireworks and more drink no doubt.

Come half past nine Sandy and Barnsey made off up the hill, with the Old Man telling them not to light the fire until they saw the first rocket go up. George and me would have gone up to light the bonfire but we wanted to see and maybe light some fireworks. Bob Telfer had brought the fireworks up from Ferniclough and The Old Man had got a couple of buckets of sand from behind the new Byre to set the fireworks in. They set the two galvanized buckets down about twenty yards inside the field opposite the Leys and folks started gathering on the road, ready for the big display.

The Old Man and Bob were like a couple of kids as the prepared the display and then they started handing everyone sparklers, saying not to light them until the first rocket had been fired, then all hell can be let loose.

There was one minute to go and the countdown was on, five, four, three, two, one, go, Dad lit the Rocket and stood back and then it went off right up in the sky. Just like a rocket George said, as we all started trying to light our sparklers, with Bob Telfer and Dad letting of all sorts of fireworks, like Roman Candles and Whirligigs, Squibs and all sorts of things and in the excitement we all forgot about the bonfire on the top of the hill. All of a sudden, someone shouted the Bonfire was alight and sure enough it was well alight and you could see the silhouettes of Barnsey and Sandy at the top of the hill. After about half an hour, the fireworks had run out and the bonfire on top of the hill had lost its intensity and folks gradually started to make their way back to their homes.

All in all, it had gone well, although George and me weren't allowed to light any fireworks and the sparklers were a bit feeble but the women folks seemed to like them.

Old Nell

Nell was a good dog. A working dog and a pet. But when she had the pups she took a funny turn. We didn't find her lair for a couple of days, until she was spotted skulking out of a loose box that was being used as a store for hay and straw. It was there that we found the dark secret. There had been some chickens go missing over the last week and there were two dead ones in the loose box. It was the early 50's and we still had rationing cards. Anything to do with food was taken seriously and these chickens meant something.

My Dad was not pleased. He took the spade. Went to the edge of the wood and dug a hole about two feet deep. On finishing he stuck the spade firmly in the loamy earth beside the hole, pressing it home with his boot. He then marched into the loose box, got some binder twine for a lead and took Nell and tied her to the spade. He then got the 12 bore and shot her. I didn't know he was going to do it and it gave me a big fright.

A loud bang. Blue smoke. She fell dead into the hole. He put the gun down, undid the binder twine from the spade and tossed it into the hole with Nell and started filling it in. She just lay there, gradually being covered. Just a nose, a tail and an open eye. Finally, disappearing under the loamy earth. He patted the loose earth flat with the back of the spade. He then turned. Gave me the spade, picked up the gun and ejected the cartridge case, saying,

"If she kills one hen, she'll kill more. There's no other way." He then went to the loose box, got the pups, all 6 of them, put them in a hessian sack with a couple stones, tied the top of the sack and dropped them into the sheep dip.

They sank slowly at first. You could hear them squeaking and see them wriggling in the sack before it disappeared under the green slimy water. We stood there watching until the bubbles stopped. He then pulled the sack out and walked over to the midden, emptying their lifeless bodies into the slurry, covering them with muck and straw.

The wind got up and it started to rain. It was a sad day. I would miss old Nell. I went to my bedroom and cried. The wind howled and I eventually looked out of the window to the small wood where Nell lay. The wood protected the farm Steadings and house from the prevailing winds. Maybe it would shelter Nell, I thought. The branches on the trees were threshing about and small birds plummeted in the violent gusts. I was mesmerized by the continuous movement. It was like looking at the flames and glowing embers in an open fire. As dusk approached, the wind abated. I went down to the wood to see old Nell and as I looked at her grave, coldness grasped the air. The shires in the stable neighed and stamped their hooves. The hens cackled. Something was awry. Evil stalked the wood that night and the eyes of the night knew, as Old Nell had known. But *we* didn't know, until the next day, when two more chickens were found dead.

The new Laird

The old folks were talking about moving and how much better it would be if we went down to England and got a farm on the flat, where the land was rich and loamy. Dad had worked there during the War and knew. George and me didn't want to move down to England. We were quite happy where we were. There're an awful lot of folks down there.

None the less, when the Old Man gets a bee in his bonnet, it is only a matter of time before something happens. Things carried on as normal for a wee while and then one day, when we came down the hill from rabbiting, there was a great big car sitting in the yard. That's when we realized things were going to change. The man who owned the car was walking around as though he owned the place, which wasn't surprising because when we saw him shake hands with Dad, he did. The deal had been done. They had shook hands on it and that was that. There was no turning back.

Barnsey the herdsman was at the byre door looking a bit bewildered and Sandy Carson had stopped sharpening the reaper blades. Mum and Aunty May were looking out of the kitchen door. George and me just stood in the yard. Chips the terrier stopped barking. Normally he barked at everything but for some reason he didn't bark at this chap but cowered instead, keeping his distance An uneasy silence crept over the yard. Barnsey sort of flipped his hair back with a look of disgust. Sandy just stood there puffing on his fag. Because they knew, as everybody else knew, you couldn't mess with the new Laird. Things were about to change. George and me looked at one another. This was the end of an era. Soon we would be off to Northamptonshire.

The Homecoming

It had been 58 years since I had last lived here. As I walked up the lane towards the old farmhouse and Steadings, memories flooded back of a happy family home in the early 50s in southern Scotland.

I had a lump in my throat at the thought of those memories and of the things we had done and the people we had known, most of them long gone but fondly remembered. I started to recall all the different things that had happened as I sat on the old style that led into the paddock. There was a strong autumn breeze blowing through the silver birch trees and beech hedges that lined the lane. It was shivering their leaves, dislodging the odd one. The bilious clouds cast their shadows like spirits as they raced from hill to hill and on towards the sea, entrapping me in a trance as I sat there.

I went back in time and all my family and friends were there. I could see the cows, the sheep and the old dogs, the old tractors, the steam engine and the old threshing machine. I could smell the vivid smells that go with all the work of a farm. People too numerous to mention. I could feel the warmth of the welcome.

But the dream ended and once again, reality prevailed and the ghosts of the past were gone. I stood up and gazed around and I could feel a presence. The rustling trees, or dashing clouds, or whatever. It was a kind presence and I knew I would be welcome here again

I started to walk down the lane to the road, to where I had parked my car and on reaching it, glanced back to where my past lay. An invisible force, like a giant hand, grabbed my heart and twisted and as my body spasmed, a tear emerged from the corner of my eye and only I knew the reason why.

For in the back waters of my mind, the past had lain dormant, until aroused by a distant memory, for a few seconds, I went back in time. To a treasured sentimental time, where sadness and happiness gelled.

A letter I wished I'd sent

Dear Aunty May,

The other day I found a letter you wrote some time ago. It ended, Love Aunty May. PS. Write soon xxx

Unfortunately this letter of mine is not soon enough.

I have written you many times in my mind and reminisced of happier days. You would have recalled many years have come and gone, since we last embraced in fond farewell, amidst our folks and kin.

You said in your letter, that things are fine. And folks come around from time to time, for a chat and a cup of tea and often ask about me. That's nice, to be remembered. I see you kept up with the local gossip, which abounds up there.

A new vicar has come to the parish. I wonder if he comes up to scratch in Aunty Ena's eyes. God help him. Cousin Ian has a new job, with a car thrown in. That will please Margaret.

I sat down the other day to rest my feet and let my mind wander down life's street. I thought of the folks from way back then when time meandered. There weren't many days went by without some fun, especially when we were young. You would remember the day you cooked the hen but forgot to gut it. I can still see Dad's face when he started to cut it. God it did pong. At least you had remembered to pluck it.

But time waits for nowt and rushes on. And it won't be long before they're all gone. All the folks who make up a life that we take for granted for most of our time.

As I read your letter the other day, I thought, God bless you, Aunty May.

With Love

Alan

The Telfers Boggy back o'er the Hill Wood

We venture full of anticipation
On and on over field and hill
To an occasional, distant curlew's shrill
Eager to be first to find old nests
Ravaged and exposed by late autumn's fearsome winds
And all the things, that winter brings
We arrive at the Telfers boggy back oer the hill wood
Where trees have died and with bleached white bark
Less lifeless limbs, skeletonised stand
An old crow's nest, in a tree branch fork, abandoned
Clumps of half frozen ferns and lichen
And a carpet of broken rotten twigs

That under foot make noises like dull fire crackers
Woodlice scamper to flee their now upturned domain
We do not stop to microscopically look
To see what has been crushed under foot
You see things in late autumn's wake
That springtime's cloaks of foliage do conceal.
The gentle springtime when things are born
And green leaves rustle in the breeze
Those days are now long gone
With winter knocking on the door
Droppings and pee marks line the floor
Leaves have long abandoned their trees
And left a beauty for the beholder's eye
That in the springtime you never spy
An early winter's ice cold mist
That clings to the ground like an earth bound shroud
A full moon rises in an explosion of light
Allowing us to see sometimes what prowls at night
Or hear more likely a sound,
A crashing, a squeal, a distant flurry
Of some poor animal that's just become quarry
Whether it's fox, stoat or weasel
They all have a way to set their table
And in this ghostly dark and deadly wood
The rule of law is for the fit and able
And as homeward we set our sights
A flock of geese in formation fly
Heading south in a clear night sky
And if you stand and silent be
There is a vast stillness of the night
And a gaggling can be heard from way up high
In a clear starry and moonlit sky
Yes way up high where geese do fly.

Printed by Amazon Italia Logistica S.r.l.
Torrazza Piemonte (TO), Italy

15898583R00064